Broken and Beautiful

By:

Brooke St. James

No part of this book may be used or reproduced in any form or by any means without prior written permission of the author.

Copyright © 2016

Brooke St. James

All rights reserved.

Other titles available from Brooke St. James:

Another Shot:
A Modern-Day Ruth and Boaz Story

When Lightning Strikes

Something of a Storm (All in Good Time #1)
Someone Someday (All in Good Time #2)

Finally My Forever (Meant for Me #1)
Finally My Heart's Desire (Meant for Me #2)
Finally My Happy Ending (Meant for Me #3)

Shot by Cupid's Arrow

Dreams of Us

Meet Me in Myrtle Beach (Hunt Family #1)
Kiss Me in Carolina (Hunt Family #2)
California's Calling (Hunt Family #3)
Back to the Beach (Hunt Family #4)
It's About Time (Hunt Family #5)

Loved Bayou (Martin Family #1)
Dear California (Martin Family #2)
My One Regret (Martin Family #3)

Chapter 1

"I don't want to get all heavy or anything," I said, "—at least not right off the bat like this." I paused and sighed. "I don't really even know why I came here. I'm not the type of person who usually likes to talk about things. You know, my feelings or whatever."

The lady, a round woman in her fifties with a head full of curly, blonde and grey hair, smiled at me from the doorway of her office. She motioned for me to come toward her, which I was already in the process of doing. I stepped past her with a smile and nod, and she closed the door behind us, all the while wearing that same welcoming smile.

"How about we start with introductions," she said as we crossed the room together.

Her office was larger than I expected. There was an area toward the back with an oversized desk, but she stopped short of that in a seating area that felt much like a formal living room. There was a couch and a couple of leather chairs surrounding a coffee table. She took a seat in one of the chairs, and glanced up at me like she was waiting for me to join her.

"You can sit anywhere you like," she said.

"I don't need to get all deep or anything," I said as I sat down on the couch. "I don't know what you normally do, but I—"

"You're Claire," she said, doing me a favor by cutting me off.

"Claire, yes. Yes ma'am."

"And you're a graphic designer."

"I'm more of an illustrator at heart, but yes ma'am, I work as a graphic designer, mostly."

She smiled and nodded like she thought that was an interesting profession. "I'm Ginger," she said.

I knew what her name was. I had seen it right on her business card. I smiled inwardly at the fact that she actually looked like Ginger. She was Ginger personified. Her entire outfit was made up of gold and tan tones, and with her hair being blonde and silver like it was, well, she was certainly representative of the name. She was even shaped a bit round and nubby like a Ginger root. I remembered we were supposed to be making introductions, so I waved and smiled, fearing that, as a therapist, she could somehow see or hear what I was thinking. I tried to think of anything besides the fact that she looked like a big, smiling Ginger root.

"I like your painting," I said, glancing at the wall behind me where there was a huge landscape painting. It was a bayou scene, which didn't surprise me since we lived in New Orleans and bayou art was everywhere. I had grown up in a rural area about an hour south of there, so scenes like the one in her painting looked like home to me.

"Thank you," she said. "It's a Benoit (ben-waa)."

He was a local artist, and I smiled and nodded, hoping if I pretended to be calm everything would be over with and I could go home.

"What made you call?" she asked.

I glanced at her as I let out a little humorless laugh. "I was just wondering that same thing."

She smiled, leaning back in her chair as if sitting around this coffee table in my company was the most comfortable place she could imagine being. She was doing everything she could to make me feel more at home, and it still wasn't working.

"I don't really know why I made this appointment," I said with a sigh. "I think it was a mistake. I'm really a happy person. I don't think I should be here." I shook my head, feeling frustrated with myself for not being able to speak without my voice coming out shaky and uncertain. I had no business getting therapy. I had no idea what I was doing. This was a huge mistake.

"What was the sequence of events that happened to make you call, Claire? Something led up to you picking up your phone. What was it?"

I sighed, hesitating. "I, uh…" I closed my eyes and shook my head, feeling silly for admitting the truth. I was scared to do anything else since she likely had some secret therapist powers and knew what I was thinking, anyway. "I thought it had to do with God or whatever," I said. "I was worried about some things, and I started thinking about God, and the next thing I knew, your card was being thrust into my hand."

"Who handed it to you?" she asked.

I shook my head and shrugged. "Some guy on the street. He thought I dropped it, and he just thrust it into my hands. I didn't even get a look at him. I'd been standing there, thinking about some things and wondering if I should talk to someone about them when he did that. I looked down and saw your card. It had that little cross on it, and—"

"You thought it was a sign from God," she said, filling in the blank when I hesitated.

"I guess," I agreed, feeling embarrassed.

"Maybe it was," she said. "I wouldn't put anything past God."

I sighed again, still not feeling confident with my choice to be there.

"What were you thinking about when the guy handed you the card?" she asked.

"My roommate," I said. "Sam. She's gonna be moving out in a couple of months."

"Will it affect your income?" she asked.

I shook my head. "We'll have no problem renting the room. Lilly's already got somebody in mind. It's not that." I paused and sighed again. "It's just that Sam's moving out because she's getting married. My best friend's getting married soon, too." I hesitated again. "I'm twenty-five, and most of my friends are either in serious relationships or are already married."

"Twenty-five is young," she said.

I grinned and shook my head as I leaned back onto the couch, running a hand through my hair. "I knew you were gonna say that, because I'm coming across like I think I need to get married tomorrow or something, which I don't. I just don't really know if I want to get married at all. You know, like ever. I'm not really interested in it. I think that might be a problem."

"Some people choose that lifestyle," she said. She tilted her head at me and stared at me with a curious gaze. "But it seems like you wouldn't be here if you were ultimately comfortable with that."

I thought about that for a few seconds. "I guess you're right," I said. "I guess deep down, I want a normal life with a husband and kids or whatever." I shivered and shook my head, smiling at her. "See? Even saying the word *husband* sounds weird coming out of my mouth." I paused, thinking she'd say something, but she just sat there, waiting for me to gather my thoughts and continue. "I think I'm scared I'll wind up being single—that I'll turn out just like my mom."

She picked up a legal pad from the coffee table and held it just long enough to scribble something on it before putting it down again. "Tell me about your mom," she said.

I should have known she would ask this question after I brought up my mother, but I still had to think about what I should say to describe her. "She's had a lot of boyfriends over the years," I said. "She drinks a lot. I don't think she's an alcoholic or anything, but she drinks quite a bit. She's always managed to hold down a job and pay her bills and everything, but she barely scrapes by most months and complains a lot in the process. I help her out as much as I can, but I've got my own responsibilities, and I just don't feel right about making her too dependent on me. She's fine, and it's not a strained relationship or anything... I'd just prefer not to end up like her."

"Do you have any siblings?" Ginger asked.

"A brother, Micah. He's eight years older than me. He lives in Metairie, but he works offshore, and he's gone a lot. He's got a good heart. He'd do anything for me, but he's got troubles of his own."

"Did you ever have a father in the picture?"

I shook my head. "Me and Micah had different dads. He got to know his dad a little bit over the years. I think they maybe even still see each other sometimes, but not me. My mom heard through a friend that my dad died a few years back, and she told me about it, but it didn't really mean much to me. I mean, I never even met the guy."

The words that came out of my mouth were, "*It didn't really mean much to me*," but my body betrayed me, and tears sprang to my eyes. I blinked, trying to hold them back.

The living, breathing Ginger root, handed me a box of tissues that had been sitting on the coffee table. I let out a laugh as I leaned forward to take one. "I promised myself there'd be no crying," I said, still holding back the tears.

Ginger gasped in mock horror. "Why would you *ever* promise something like that?" she asked. "Crying's the best sometimes."

"I'm not sad or anything. I just get mad when I think about my dad leaving."

"Was there something your dad could have protected you from?" she asked. She phrased it as more of an assumption than a question, like she expected me to agree with it.

"Probably lots of things," I said, trying to remain vague.

"Can you name a couple?"

"Like my mom having to scrape by—having to work two jobs and depend on people for handouts."

"Who'd she depend on for handouts?" she asked.

"Whoever," I said. "The church, or my uncle, or whoever."

I felt blood rise to my cheeks when I said that. I knew it. She could see straight through me with her therapist powers.

"What happened with your uncle, Claire?" she asked with a concerned expression.

I grabbed several tissues out of the box in a hurry before putting my hands in front of my face. I knew I couldn't hide the way my face contorted with tears, but I tried my best. I dabbed at my eyes, trying to shake off the feelings that came with the memories of him.

"He was my mom's uncle," I said. "I guess that makes him my great-uncle."

Ginger nodded sweetly, as if she had already assumed the worst, and was totally fine with whatever I was about to say. She pulled a few more tissues out of the box and leaned over to hand them to me. I smiled through still-watering eyes as I took them from her. I blew my nose with the old bunch before using the fresh ones to dab my cheeks.

"I made a promise to myself that I wasn't gonna get all deep like this," I said. "And here I am, not even ten minutes in, and I'm spilling my guts. I didn't even want to talk about my uncle. I told myself I wasn't going to do it. But I guess some part of me thinks I need to get it out."

"Getting it out is always a step in the right direction," she said. "And you're not alone. People have lived through some crazy things, Claire. Why do you think I have a fresh box of tissues on the table?" She paused and used her head to motion behind her. "There are at least twenty boxes in a cabinet back there. I buy them in bulk."

I offered a smile, but glanced to the side of her, not knowing what to say next.

"Was it sexual?" she asked.

I was still and silent for several seconds before nodding. "He didn't... I mean, we didn't... I, uh... he never did anything to me, or anything. He just sort of made me do some..." I trailed off and let out a disgusted sigh, shaking my head. "I don't even know why I'm telling you all this. It's not a big deal. I'm fine. I turned out fine. I would never do that kind of thing to anyone else, and that's all that matters. I have no weird sexual stuff—other than disinterest."

"Was this one incident, Claire, or multiple?"

"More than one."

"More than ten?"

I shook my head. "I don't think so. It seems like it was several, but I was young, so it's hard to remember. I'm sure I blocked it."

"And as far as you remember, he never touched you?"

I shook my head.

"But he asked you to do things?"

I nodded.

"And you were too little to know any better," she continued.

I shook my head, and dabbed my cheeks as more silent tears fell from my eyes. "I must have known something was wrong, because I didn't tell my mom or my brother what he did. I don't know why I let him make me do that and I didn't tell anybody. I should have told them right when it happened. I don't know why I didn't."

I paused staring into space as I tried to remember.

"I don't even think he threatened me or anything. I don't remember anything like that. Maybe I thought the whole thing was my idea or something, maybe that's why I didn't tell anyone." I shrugged, shaking my head, trying to push it out of my mind like I'd done all these years. "It is what it is. I was a little kid. It happened, and there's nothing I can do about it now. I think I'm a pretty well-rounded person, otherwise… all except for the fact that I'm not really that interested in a relationship."

"But you said yourself that you eventually wanted marriage and a family and the whole bit."

"Eventually," I agreed.

"So, it's important that we deal with these feelings."

I gave her a small smile and looked around as if to indicate that's why I was there.

"Am I the first person you've told?" she asked.

I nodded.

"And how old do you think you were when this happened?"

I shrugged. "Five or six, I guess."

Giant, silent tears streamed down my face. They were caused by embarrassment, and anger, and a whole host of other emotions.

"And all this time, you've never told anyone?" she asked, seeming like it was hard for her to believe.

Her genuine disbelief and concern had me unable to stop crying. I just kept the stack of tissue at the top of my nose for a few seconds, wiping the corners of my eyes as the tears came streaming out.

The next thing I knew, Ginger was circling around the coffee table so she could put a comforting arm around me.

Chapter 2

"I'm not really a hugger," I said, stiffening up and patting Ginger's arm as graciously as I could. I pulled back a little, trying to get myself together and stop crying so she'd start keeping her hands to herself. "Is that part of this?" I asked, looking at her cautiously. "Hugging?"

"When I feel like it's called for," she said.

"I'm pretty sure I won't call for it," I said as sweetly as I could. "I don't think I need that."

I knew my aversion to physical contact was abnormal, so I usually tried to suck it up and hug people in greeting or whatever, but this was different. I was paying her, for goodness sake. Hugs were a barely tolerable part of my life. I certainly wasn't about to start *paying* for them.

Ginger created a little distance between us by scooting over a few inches, but she did not get off the couch. I adjusted by shifting to face her and kicking my knee onto the seat between us.

"My best friend from childhood is a big hugger," I said. "Her whole family is. Mine never was, though. I can't remember ever hugging my mom. I can't even remember the last time we touched each other, actually."

She reached out and touched the lower part of my leg, since it was closest to her. I wanted so badly to pull away or at least flinch, but I knew she was doing it as a test, so I sat very still, praying she'd take it off. After a few seconds, she did.

"How was that?" she asked.

"What?"

She glanced down at my knee. "That. My hand on your leg."

I looked around, searching for a hidden camera or something. "Is this orthodox?" I asked. "This approach you're doing... it seems a little weird."

She sat back against the corner of the couch, regarding me with a smile. "Was it that bad?" she asked.

"Your hand?"

She nodded, and I shrugged. "I just don't understand why it's necessary to touch me," I said.

"It's not necessary," she said. "But human contact is good for the soul, and I think it's healthy for you to practice it."

I shook my head. "Yeah, that's definitely not what I thought this was."

"What'd you think it was?" she asked, staring at me like she was genuinely interested to hear what I'd say.

"Talking?" I said, tentatively.

She smiled patiently. "We are talking," she said. "Tell me about your best friend, the hugger. Is she the one who's getting married?"

"Wynn, yes. She's getting married in a couple of months. I'm happy for her. I love the guy she's marrying. It's a guy we've known for years through college. They're great together. I'm happy for her. She's like a sister to me."

"And you never told her what you went through with your uncle?" she asked.

"No," I said. "I would never." I shot her a *how could you even think that* face that made her give me a contemplative smile.

"It's way more difficult to hold onto something like that than it is to share it," she said. "I'm really surprised you guarded it so tightly all these years. You would have been much better off sharing that with someone."

"Really? I asked, looking around as if I might find clues about her other clients and all of their problems and tendencies so I could compare them to my own. "What do other people do, walk around announcing that they were abused? *Was* I even abused? Is that what you call it? I mean, he didn't—"

"Yes, Claire, that's what you call it. There's no other way to describe it. You should have never been put in that position as a child, and your great uncle, God help him, will be held accountable for that. You did what most children in your situation do. You held it inside, thinking somehow that it was your fault for going along with it. By the time you were old enough to understand what happened, it felt like it was too late to tell anyone, and maybe they wouldn't have believed you, anyway. I'm not surprised that you didn't tell your best friend, especially if her family was your link to some sense of a healthy family environment."

"Oh, her family was definitely my ticket to normal. I don't know what I would have done without them. Her dad sat us both down when we were freshmen in high school. He gave us a whole talk about working toward college and setting long-term goals. He looked me in the eyes and said I'd have to work harder than the kids who had parents to pay for their college. But he told me it would be worth it. He knew my mom's situation, and he said I'd have to work my butt off in high school if I wanted any chance of earning scholarships that would pay for my college. My mom didn't teach me anything about setting goals or working toward something. She wasn't trying to be mean, she just didn't know that stuff. The Martins helped me so much. Scholarships covered most of my tuition, but Wynn's parents covered the rest. They paid for my books and some of my food, too. I really owe them a lot."

"Sounds like a nice family," she said.

"The best," I said. "Totally wonderful and normal."

She smiled and reached out to touch my knee again. "Claire," she said, looking at me sincerely. "Nobody's totally wonderful and normal. We're all sinners, baby. We all have problems, and we're all equally in need of God's grace."

I glanced down at her hand, which was still on the edge of my knee.

"Not all touch is perverted, Claire. I'm so sorry your great-uncle did that to you. What he did was wrong, and you're super tough for hanging onto it all by yourself like this."

"I know not all touch is perverted, I just don't understand why it has to be a part of what we're doing here."

She took her hand off of my knee and sat back. "Yes, but exploring your aversion to human contact is going to be key in getting to your courtship and going into a marriage." She leaned back, giving me a satisfied grin. "I think we're done. That did it. We made some really great progress today."

"Really?"

"Oh my goodness, yes. You came in saying you were keeping it surface level, and now here we are making real progress."

"What progress?" I asked. "Other than me telling you all that stuff."

"That is the progress," she said with a huge grin. "That's all you needed. It's gonna work wonders. In the coming weeks, you're gonna think back to this conversation. You're gonna think about telling me everything that happened with your mom's uncle, and then you'll remember me telling you that you're definitely capable of getting past this and having a healthy marriage and family." She smiled. "You'll remember me saying that I'd seen other clients who had gone through much worse get past their issues and go on to live totally normal, happy lives."

"You didn't say any of those things," I said.

"Oh, but they're the truth. You may have reasons to withhold your trust from men or other human beings in general, Claire, but you'll get past them, and you'll get over this. God will help you." She smiled as she patted my knee again. "You're already halfway there just by coming here and telling me this." She pulled back, looking at me with a curious glance. "Is that the thing that stands out as the most unforgivable thing of your childhood?" she asked, looking at me like she already knew the answer.

"I should hope so," I said.

She shook her head with a sad smile. "You'd be amazed at some of the things people have endured in their childhoods. My clients here in New Orleans are just a few in a whole world full of people with problems, and even still, I feel like I've heard the saddest things imaginable. You're not alone, Claire. Not even close." She stared at me as if that was all we were going to say.

"Are you gonna tell me I need to come in here every week or something?" I asked, seeing her shift to the edge of her seat on the couch. She was like a human-sized Ginger root that was repositioning, taking on the shape of another Ginger root.

"Actually, no," she said. "We did good today. You've got a lot to think about with the news that you're normal and everything."

"What do you mean normal?"

She smiled, still perched on the edge of the couch. "I mean you're normal." She used the edge of her fist to pretend to stamp the legal pad that was sitting on the coffee table in a dramatic manner. "Diagnosis normal," she said with a flourish. "No more therapy needed."

Again, I looked around the room for hidden cameras. "Seriously?" I asked.

"Seriously, Claire. You didn't come in here to become one of my regular clients. You're a very well rounded young woman. You suffered mild sexual abuse as a child, and you're coping with it beautifully. You're gonna be fine. I'd like to see you again eventually, but not right away." She smiled, and again reached out to pat my knee. "It'll be more of a *come check in and let me know how well you're doing* visit."

"So that's it?" I glanced at the legal pad, trying with no avail to see the words that were scribbled on it from earlier.

"You're fine," she said when she saw me looking.

"I'm usually not so emotional," I said, wiping the corners of my eyes to make sure there was no smeared makeup.

"I know you're not," she said. "You could probably stand to be *more* emotional, if anything."

I straightened up, sitting on the edge of the couch with her and thinking about everything she had said.

"You're welcome to call and come back next week if you feel like you need to," she said with a shrug. "But I think you'll work it out. That's what you've done all these years, and it's worked pretty well for you."

For whatever reason, Ginger earned my respect by knowing that I probably wouldn't want to come back and making that easy on me. "Thanks," I said even though her rescheduling techniques were a bit odd.

"Just go home and let it soak in that what you went through with your uncle wasn't a shock to me. And it certainly wasn't a shock to God. He's used the circumstances in your life, good and bad, to mold you into the woman you are. I can tell you have a grasp of that somewhere in there." She reached up and tapped her finger on my temple, pointing at my noggin.

I smiled shyly. "I know the events of my life have shaped me into who I am. I just didn't know if I was what you'd call *normal* since I can't really get past the two-month mark without getting totally turned off by a guy."

"You're gonna get over that," she said, nodding confidently. "You'll be fine. You just haven't found the right one… or realized him, however you want to look at it." She patted my leg before standing with a groan. "But certainly feel free to come see me again if you want to sometime."

"Thank you," I said, somewhat reluctantly as I stood up.

"Let's get you started with a hug," she said, reaching out to take me into her arms.

I hugged her back, feeling oddly more and more comfortable with it. I was thankful for the visit and everything she said while we were talking. This time, I tried to come across as huggable as I could.

"That was *great*," she said, when we broke the hug.

I laughed. "Like I said, I fake it for my friends."

She smiled. "I'm glad you consider me a friend. Now, go out there and give away about ten more of those."

I smiled. "Is that my homework?"

"Absolutely!" she said, with a huge grin. "In fact, I'm prescribing you ten hugs right now."

She held up her palm and pretended to write on a prescription pad. "Ten hugs that you initiate..." she said slowly, trailing off as she glanced up at me from her fake notepad. She pretended to rip off the piece of fake paper from her pad and hand it to me. She sat there with her hand extended, so I finally pretended to take it from her. She smiled to let me know I'd done the right thing by playing along. "Do you ever *initiate* hugs?" she asked.

"No," I said with an expression that indicated I had never been more certain of anything in my life. "Never."

"You need to go out into the world and initiate ten hugs. Roommates, friends, family, whoever. Reach out and hug the first person you see that you know."

I smiled. It was Thursday, so later that evening, I would see my trainer at the gym. Nate and I only made physical contact when absolutely necessary. He knew I liked it that way. He would not know what to think if I hugged him. He'd probably think I was hitting on him or had completely lost my mind. I laughed at the thought.

"What?" Ginger asked.

"I was thinking about hugging my trainer. That would be so awkward."

"Hug the next person you see that you know," she said.

"It'll probably be Nate. Unless Lilly's home when I go by there."

"Hug Nate then. Or Lilly. Hug both."

"Okay," I said with enough uncertainty that she knew I was skeptical of my own ability.

"You've got this, Claire. You're gonna hug people, and eventually you're gonna like a man for more than two months. You've already forgiven your uncle and your mother, now you need to choose to forget about it and move on with your life—your very normal life."

"And some guy's supposed to be okay with everything that happened to me?"

"Of course he will," she said. "And don't think you won't tell him, because when you find the right one, you'll share everything."

"That seems impossible right now," I said. "I just don't think the type of guy I want wants the type of girl I am—the type that something like that would have happened to."

She narrowed her eyes at me like she was trying to figure out what I was saying. "You're not a *type*, Claire. You're just you. You'll find somebody who loves you for exactly who you are—past and all. And it might be closer than you think." She winked at me, and then we stood there and stared at each other for a second before she said, "You better get going, sweet pea."

I walked out of that office in a bit of a daze as I tried to process all the words I had just exchanged with Ginger the highly unconventional therapist. I remembered her stamping her fist onto that notebook and scribbling onto the invisible prescription pad, and I couldn't help but smile. I stepped onto the sidewalk, grinning at what a trip she was.

"What's so funny Claire King in the boxing ring?" I heard someone say. I had been looking at the ground, but my gaze drifted upward when he spoke. I knew it was Cam Martin before I saw his face. No one else on earth had ever referred to me as *Claire King in the boxing ring*.

Chapter 3

Cam Martin was like family to me.

He was Wynn's cousin, and we all grew up in the same rural area south of New Orleans. We went way back. He called me "Claire King in the boxing ring" in reference to one time as kids when we were all on the trampoline together. Cam and his brother were trying to tickle us girls, and I stood there with my fists in the air, daring them to come near us. Cam got such a kick of me standing there like that, that he had teased me about it ever since. He and his brother also liked to call me nicknames that rhymed with my last name, so that one applied on both accounts.

I liked Cam a lot, but I hadn't seen him much during the last few years because he had been in a serious relationship with a girl who happened to be extremely jealous. She was one of those passive aggressive types who could tell you just what she thought about you without saying a word—and most of the time what she thought about you was bad... especially if you were a girl.

I instinctually stepped back from Cam, wondering if Jolene was somewhere close by, but then I remembered they had broken up. I still glanced over his shoulder just to make sure before making eye contact with him again.

He was probably the most handsome guy in all of Louisiana—maybe even the whole world. I imagined him on the cover of People's most beautiful issue with gleaming white teeth and his hair blowing in the wind. It was a warm spring day and he had on jeans with a vintage-looking Martin Outfitters T-shirt.

Steve and Mitch Martin were brothers who started the popular nationwide chain of sporting goods stores. Steve had two boys (Cole and Cam) and Mitch had three girls (Alex, Wynn, and Amelia). Cole, Cam, and Alex all worked for the family business even though they could have probably just retired early on their daddy's fortune. They were probably ka-zillionaires by now, but you'd never know by how down-to-earth they were.

"What are you doing over here?" Cam asked, reaching out to poke at my ribs. I easily dodged him because he wasn't really trying all that hard.

I looked at my surroundings, contemplating whether or not I should lie about going to a therapist. The area we were in was a mix of businesses and residential. The therapist's office looked like a house, and I had exited from the side, so Cam probably had no idea where I'd come from.

"What are you doing here?" I asked, stalling while I tried to decide what to say.

"I'm looking at some retail space for Jacob."

"For his furniture?" I asked.

Wynn's older sister, Alex, was married to a guy named Jacob who made furniture and kitchen items from all sorts of expensive wood.

"He's got Caleb working with him full time," Cam said. "They've been doing all their business online, but they're thinking about putting some of their stuff in that store over there."

"It's nice," I said. "I've been in there a few times. Jacob's stuff would be a good fit." I pointed at the opposite corner. "That café's really good, too. Have you been to it?"

Cam looked over his shoulder and then back at me, shaking his head.

"You should check it out sometime," I said.

"You hungry?" he asked.

"Me? I'm…" I glanced down at my watch. "It's only four o'clock." I stared at him, wondering if he'd even been serious when he asked that, and he smiled like he enjoyed watching me fidget.

"Yeah, what are you doing over here at this time of day?" he asked. "I thought you worked downtown."

"I do. I'm over here at an appointment."

"What kind?" he asked.

"None of your beeswax," I said, widening my eyes at him, which made him laugh.

"Must be a shrink if you won't tell me."

"What?" I asked in utter disbelief.

"It's okay," he said. "I won't tell anybody I saw you over here at your shrink's office."

I knew he was totally kidding with me, but I couldn't resist the opportunity to make him feel bad.

"I was seeing a therapist," I said. I happened to be a gifted actress—I had always been that way. I had no problems saying the most outlandish things with a straight face. I made a sad, withdrawn expression as I stared down, shaking my head. "Please don't tell anyone you saw me over here."

"Seriously?" he asked. He stared at me with sweet concern, leaning over to force me to stare into his dark brown eyes even though I tried to look away. I remained stoic for several seconds before cracking a smile.

Cam shook his head at me, smiling. "You made me feel bad for a second."

"You should still feel bad, you big oaf," I said, pushing at his shoulder. "I seriously was over here going to a therapist." I pointed at the blue house behind us. "It's not as dramatic as I said, but I really was with a therapist. That's her office right there."

"Are you serious right now?" he asked, obviously mortified by the fact that he had teased me.

I couldn't help but laugh at his expression. "Yeah, but it's no big deal. It was my first time to go to her, and I'm not going back or anything."

"Why? Was she a quack or something?"

I laughed. "I don't think so," I said, not sounding so sure of myself. "She just told me I didn't need to come back. She said I was normal."

Cam began coughing, like hearing the word *normal* in reference to me made him uncontrollably choke. He was joking around again, and I narrowed my eyes at him and made a fifth-grade expression telling him to be quiet. Cam looked at the blue house as if trying to figure something out. "Did she seriously say you were normal?" he asked. "In those words?"

"Is that so hard to believe?" I asked, crossing my arms indignantly.

Cam laughed. "Yes, Claire, it is. Normal is not at all the word I would use to describe you. In fact, it's one of the words I'd particularly try to *avoid* when describing you."

A lady came walking down the sidewalk, and Cam and I stepped to the side to get out of her way.

"What words would you use, Cameron?"

He shrugged. "Quirky, artsy, musical, cute, weird, quiet, talented, beautiful, picky, shy, artistic—" Cam ticked off words one by one and showed no signs of stopping. I was so totally thrown off by hearing the word *beautiful*, that I nearly choked for real.

"That's good," I said, cutting him off as I coughed. "I didn't know you'd start reading out of the adjective dictionary."

"There's no such thing as an adjective dictionary," he said, "and those were all genuine ways I'd describe you."

"Weird?" I asked.

He smiled and shrugged.

A couple passed us on the sidewalk, and Cam reached out to put a hand on my shoulder so he could make sure we were out of their way. By instinct, I shrugged out of his grasp as quickly but politely as possible. This time it was a little different, though. This time, I didn't hate having his hand on there so much. I wondered if it was possible that I was already making progress. I swallowed hard, trying to make sense of all my thoughts. I glanced at the blue house, wondering who that Ginger lady was and what in the world had just happened to me.

"Yes, weird, Claire. You're weird. You wouldn't be friends with my cousin if you weren't. I meant it in a good way." Cam noticed me looking at the house, and he gestured toward it. "I'm glad you got a good prognosis, though," he said.

"Me too," I said. I stared blankly at his arm as I remembered some of the things she said. "I'm not even really sure what happened to me in there, or who that lady was. I don't think she's a doctor or anything. She's just a therapist." I sighed, making eye contact with him. "I don't even know. That was crazy. Part of me thinks she was a genius, and the other part is like *what the heck just happened in there?*" I stared at Cam with an expression that said I didn't even believe what was about to come out of my mouth. "She wrote a prescription for ten hugs on a fake note pad and peeled it off and pretended to hand it to me."

Cam regarded me with a completely confused expression like he was genuinely trying to make sense of what I was saying. "She what?" he asked, finally.

I let out a little laugh at the ridiculousness of it. I already kind of regretted saying it the first time, so hesitated to say it a second. I shook my head as if brushing it off as I said, "She told me to go hug ten people."

"I thought that's what you said," Cam said, smiling at me. "Did you say she wrote a prescription for hugs on a *fake note pad*?"

I nodded. "And then she pretended to hand it to me."

He smiled. "What'd you do?"

"I pretended to take it from her."

His smiled broadened as he glanced at the house. "What are you supposed to do now?" he asked, focusing on me again.

"I'm supposed to hug my trainer, Nate, when I see him tonight, and then I have to hug the next nine people after that. She said I should work on my human contact."

"You do need to work on that," Cam said. He reached out to poke my ribs, and I instinctually stepped back and held up a fist.

He let out a laugh. "See? You truly are Claire King in the boxing ring."

"I am not," I said. "It's just because you always try to tickle me."

"I'm not trying to tickle you," he said. "I was just touching you."

"On my ribs." I said, looking down at my side. "That's where you touch someone to tickle them."

"I wasn't going to tickle you."

"Well, it looked like it."

"Why do you gotta karate chop me?" he asked. "Why don't I get to be one of those ten people you have to hug for your prescription?"

Cam Martin was devastatingly gorgeous. He'd always been the most popular guy we knew growing up, and that hadn't changed as we became adults. Everyone loved him. He was a New Orleans boy through and through, and people often teased him about running for political office even though he had no desire or plans to do so.

"Does it have to be a certain ten people?" he asked when I didn't respond to his first question right away.

"No," I said. "And I'm relatively sure I don't have to do it *at all* since I'm not going back there." I looked at the house. "Maybe I wasn't even *in* there," I said, thinking out loud. "Maybe that whole visit was a dream."

"It must have been if she called you normal," he said, making us both laugh.

"It was good seeing you, Wynn's cousin," I said teasing him with a smile and a wave as I turned to walk away.

He screwed up his face at me before looking toward the side and holding his arms out like he intended for me to walk right into them.

I laughed, feeling nervous and anxious at the sight of him standing there like that. I wasn't sure if I had ever hugged Cam. I was sure I had in a casual way over the years, but this felt very official. He motioned with his hands for me to come into his arms and I just stood there, shaking my head and giggling nervously.

"Claire, it's not that hard. Take two steps toward me."

I took one, and as soon as I did, he took a step toward me, closing the distance between us, and wrapping his big arms all the way around my shoulders. He enveloped me like a warm cocoon. The urge to push away was overwhelming, but I knew Cam. He was a Martin, and I knew he'd make me stand there and hug him until he thought I'd sufficiently done my homework. I sighed, resting the side of my face on his chest as he held there.

"Claire," he said, leaning over to speak near my ear.

"What?" I asked.

"This does not count."

"What?" I asked innocently. I pulled back far enough to glance up at him and then down at my arms, which were strategically planted between us. I hadn't meant to do it, but my fists were under my chin and I had gone into the hug in a sort of flattened-out boxing pose with my arms folded between us. Cam and I both looked down at my fists and then at each other. We both smiled.

"That was totally a hug," I said, shimmying away from him as his grip loosened.

He shook his head as if to say he was really disappointed with me and honestly a bit surprised that I was unable to do it correctly.

"That's not a hug *at all*, Claire. To make it a hug, you have to put your arms around me instead of using them as a barricade."

"Yeah, but you were hugging me," I said. "That counts."

"You weren't hugging me back."

"I was hugging you my own way."

"Elbows first?" He smiled and shook his head again. "I didn't get a thing out of that. That was all take and no give on your part." He was teasing me again, and I narrowed my eyes at him.

"Fine, we'll do it," I said.

He shook his head and raised his hands in surrender. "Hey, nobody's making you do anything. I was just trying to help you with your recovery."

"It's not recovery," I said.

"Sure it is," he said. "From huglessness."

"Huglessness? That's not even a word."

"It should be," he said. "Suffering from huglessness?" he added in a hilarious, dramatic imitation of a TV commercial. "Come to the crazy lady in the blue house on St. Charles and get your prescription hugs. Act now and Cam Martin will be standing on the sidewalk to offer your first."

I laughed, shaking my head at him for being such a goofball. "I'm doing it, and then I'm forgetting this whole thing ever happened. Can you please just forget it too?"

"Why don't you like me, Claire?" he asked. His usually light-hearted expression turned a little serious, and I pulled back, wondering what exactly he meant by that.

"Ever since we were kids, you've been keeping a certain distance from me."

"That's a distance I keep from everybody," I said. "Not just you."

He stared at me for a second, looking right into my eyes. "No wonder she wrote that prescription," he said.

I shrugged. "I'm just not a hugger," I said, not knowing why either of them thought it was a big deal.

"Maybe today you are," he said.

I smiled. "Maybe so."

Chapter 4

"Okay," Cam said in an instructional tone with a physical stance like he was about to give me some sort of plan. "I'm gonna step toward you and put my arms around you just like I did a minute ago... only this time, you'll open yours and grab onto me." He paused and gestured to his mid-section. "Put your arms around here."

I narrowed my eyes at him again. "I know how to hug," I said.

He smiled. Cam was the type of person who smiled all the time, so it shouldn't have taken me off guard, but it did. I usually wasn't the direct recipient of one of Cam's smiles. Not that he didn't like me, because he did... we got along fine. It's just that usually, at family functions, I just hung out with Wynn and her sisters.

I had been purposefully trying to ignore Cole and Cam for most of my life. They were super-popular jock types, and I had mostly just hung out with the artsy crowd so I could specifically avoid people like them. It's not that they tried to make me feel inferior or anything, but I guess maybe I was afraid they would if I gave them the chance. We had countless encounters over the years, but he was correct when he said I kept a certain distance.

"Show me, then," Cam said in an almost challenging tone.

"Show you what?" I asked, since I'd been lost in thought and forgotten what we were talking about.

"That you know how to hug."

"Fine," I said. I took a step toward him and closed my eyes (almost cringing a little) as I latched onto him. I couldn't help but marvel at the firmness of his torso. I'd hugged other guys in my life, including my brother, but Cam had a certain muscular feel I'd never experienced before. He was lean, but he was somehow thick with muscle at the same time. I was thinking all this as I hugged him, but soon I became distracted by his chest, which was now shaking.

"What?" I asked, looking up at him once it hit me that he was laughing.

"You. You braced yourself like you were about to squeeze the living daylights out of me, and now you're barely even touching me."

I squeezed a little tighter, looking at him as if wondering if this was now acceptable.

"Tighterrrr," he whispered dramatically, being the clown he was.

I squeezed a little tighter. "Still tighter," he whispered, looking displeased with my efforts.

I abandoned looking at him in favor of resting my face on his chest. I squeezed him tightly, knowing he wouldn't be satisfied until I went ahead and did it. He drew me further into his arms, wrapping me up securely. We hugged each other for what must have been ten full seconds before I pulled back.

"There," I started to say, but I cut off when Cam pulled me against him again. I knew he was just being Cam and giving me a hard time about my *hug homework*, but I hugged him again anyway.

It didn't feel all that bad, really. Maybe it was just because I was comfortable with Cam and I trusted him. I thought of my trainer, and knew I could never see myself standing there hugging him for ten seconds straight like I was doing with Cam.

"I'm pretty sure we've never done that before," Cam said a few seconds later as I let go of him and stepped back. He regarded me curiously like I was made of a mysterious substance. He shifted around, putting a hand to his chest. "You made my heart beat fast on that one, Claire."

I laughed, and reached out to push at his shoulder. "You're funny," I said.

"I think you're the one who's being funny," he said.

"What'd I do?" I asked, shrugging.

"I'm not sure, really," he said still staring at me like it was the first time we ever met.

"Cam," I said, snapping my fingers one time to get his attention.

"That was good," he said, patting my shoulder and getting back to being Wynn's cousin again. "I'm glad you were normal at your doctor's visit. I'm pretty sure the hugs are working. That was good. You did good."

I smiled and shook my head at Cam as I put my hand up for a high five. He slapped my hand. It was at that moment, that I realized I enjoyed physical contact with Cam Martin. Not that anything would actually work out between he and I, but at least I wasn't cringing at a man's touch. This was a good sign.

"What?" he asked, seeing me smile.

"Nothing."

"You wanna hug again?" he asked.

I smiled. "No."

"Why not?" he asked with a shrug.

"Because we already did."

"Fair enough," he said with a nod. He gestured to the large, locally owned store that was a few doors down from where we were standing. "Do you wanna come with me to check out that retail space for Jacob?"

"I know it's nice," I said. "It'll be perfect for Jacob's stuff."

"I thought you might want to walk with me, you know, just for fun."

"Ohhh, like just two pals hanging out, walking down the block."

He smiled. "Yep, just two pals," he said as he turned. I fell into stride beside him, and we began walking toward Keller's.

"I'll walk with you and maybe peek my head in, but I have to go in a minute. I have a workout scheduled.

"Personal trainer?" Cam asked.

I shrugged. "Not because I want to or because I'm fancy or anything. I'm just too lazy to stick with anything if I don't have someone staying on me, holding me accountable. Nate will just about drive over to my house if I don't show up. I need that."

"Nate Pilgreen," Cam assumed, since he knew every one in New Orleans.

"How do you know Nate?" I asked even though I wasn't surprised.

"He helped out with some of the training when I was playing football."

"Tulane?" I asked.

Cam nodded.

I'd been to some of his football games over the years, but it was so rough that I could barely stand to watch. I was always afraid they'd get hurt.

"Nate'll getcha if you don't stay in line," Cam said.

"I know. That's why I can't hang out too much longer. I still have to run home before I go."

"You don't have to stay," he said as we approached the turn in the sidewalk where the path led to Keller's. He stopped there, thinking I'd say goodbye.

"I'll come in and see the space," I said, since for whatever reason, I felt like hanging out with him. "I have a few minutes."

"Well, come on," he said. He turned, and took my hand, placing it on the inside of his arm. The maneuver was very smooth and practiced, and I smiled inwardly, thinking he was accustomed to having a woman on his arm.

I kept my hand around his upper arm as we walked up the path to the door and into Keller's. My fingertips kept registering the feel of his bicep, which translated to an increased heart rate. I tried to pull away once we got inside, but Cam put his other hand over mine to stop me from taking it away.

We walked through the showroom floor to a secluded area in the corner, which would be the designated space for Jacob's stuff. "It'll be perfect with this window over here," I said, pulling my hand out from under Cam's arm once we had stopped walking and were standing in the middle of the room. I glanced at him when I stepped away to see if he'd react to me pulling away, but he just watched me with an amused grin.

"I'm just gonna call you Claire from now on," he said.

"Why?" I asked with a disappointed frown.

"Because all those names were for a little girl, and you're all grown up."

"I am not all grown up," I said, pushing at his shoulder. "You should see my room. I've got about a hundred work-in-progress comics and sketches scattered about. I'd hardly give me credit for being grown up. The boxing ring thing's fine. It does make me feel like I'm ten again, and probably brings back some trauma, but that's no problem."

"Do you seriously have trauma from Claire King in the boxing ring?" he asked.

I laughed. "No, Cam. I'm fine with you calling me boxing ring, or silly thing, or any of the other nicknames that rhyme with my last name."

"I know you're fine with it, but I just want to call you Claire."

"You can call me whatever you like, Cameron," I said in a playfully dramatic tone since he was getting serious on me.

Cam stared at me, scanning my face. I watched as his eyes roamed from my eyes down to my mouth. "Claire, don't you go saying my name like that," he said.

He was serious when he said it. I was normally a great actress who could carry on a charade with the best of them, but I couldn't do it this time.

I let out a little nervous laugh. "You don't like me saying, Cameron Reese Martin?" I asked.

"Claaaire," he said, still staring straight at me. "Don't."

"Don't what?"

"Don't say my name like that."

I giggled, but he didn't laugh back. There was a faint smile on his face, and I couldn't help but stare at it. "Don't say your name?" I asked.

He shook his head, still wearing that easy smile. "No," he said. "Don't."

"Why not?" I asked stubbornly, since I'd never been a fan of conforming to rules.

"Because it made me feel some type of way."

"What type of way is that?" I asked.

"A way that I probably shouldn't," he said, staring at me as if he was considering a number of possibilities.

"Cam are you trying to get fresh with me?" I asked, snapping my fingers in front of him again.

His smile grew when I did that.

"You're staring at me like you're about to kiss me or something," I said.

"I know it's weird," he said dazedly. "I'm pretty much feeling like I want to."

"To what?" I asked.

"To do that," he said.

I was fairly certain he was referring to kissing me but I didn't have time to ask because someone walked into the room.

"Mr. Martin, I see you've found the spot," a man said, striding into the room where we were standing.

"We did," Cam said, turning to greet the man with a smile.

"I'll let you two have at it," I said as the guy approached. I stepped away from Cam, and when I did, an odd, electrical, zapping, stabbing sensation went through my chest and even my neck and jaw. I didn't want to leave him, which was extremely weird for me.

Cam looked at me with a smile, but there was a sincere edge to it. "You sure?" he asked. "I won't be long here. We could check out that—"

"I'm sure," I said gesturing to the man, who was fast approaching. "I'm gonna let you get on with your meeting. I have to get to the gym, anyway. You know Nate."

"Okay," he said, though he didn't seem quite satisfied.

"This is a great space," I said, offering my two cents about the store as I stepped around the approaching man. "Bye," I added, waving at the man and then at Cam. "It was nice seeing you."

"Nice seeing you too, Claire. You going to Wynn's wedding?"

I smiled and nodded since we both knew that was a silly question. "Are you?" I asked, being equally as silly.

He shot me a slow, sideways smile. "I guess I'll see you there," he said.

There was some sort of unspoken promise in his words that had my heart beating faster than normal.

"Okay," I said, even though that was two months away and it wasn't even on my radar at the moment considering everything I'd just rehashed with the therapist. "Bye," I said.

"Bye," Cam said.

I smiled casually again and waved at them both before finding the door. I crossed that store and went out onto the sidewalk feeling like I was in one huge dream. The whole appointment with Ginger followed by my encounter with the Camtinental Express left me feeling a bit overwhelmed. I left that place trying to make sense of everything that had just happened.

One-after-another, I had flashbacks of my meeting with Ginger (who might or might not be some sort of genius) and of my run-in with Cam. I thought back to the way he looked at me, and knew it was a way he'd never looked at me before. My stomach tied into a knot at the memory of it.

Chapter 5
Two months later

"Oh my goodness, Claire, I was so excited to see your name on my books this morning!"

I had almost talked myself into believing that Ginger, the therapist, didn't even exist, but there she was, smiling at me from behind her round glasses.

She met me when I first stepped into her office, and she took me into her arms right away, which I wasn't really expecting. She gave me a squeeze, testing me out.

"Oh, you're doing so well!" she said, obviously happy with the improvements in my hugability. She pulled back to stare at me. "I knew you'd do fine," she said. A serious look crossed her face as she reached up and pinched my cheek like an aunt would do when you see her at Christmas. "What in the world took you so long?" she asked, with a teasing grin. She gestured with a flick of her chin for me to follow her. "I thought you'd be back after a couple of weeks or so."

I gave her a confused expression as I sat in the corner of the couch and she took a seat in the chair closest to me. "You might be thinking of someone else. When I left here, you told me not to worry about coming back. I only did today because I wanted to ask you a question."

"Shoot," she said, leaning back in her chair with a sweet smile.

"My uncle."

She nodded.

It took me a few seconds, but I said, "He died the other day."

She nodded again but otherwise waited for me to continue.

"My mom called me like a week before it happened. She said Uncle Todd was getting bad and asked if I wanted to come see him."

"And did you go?" she asked.

After a few seconds, I shook my head. "No." I paused and sighed before continuing. "I just didn't want to," I said. "He was sick and old, and he probably wouldn't even recognize me, anyway." Some tears sprang to my eyes, and I did my best to hold them back as I stared at the trusty tissue box on the coffee table. I glanced at Ginger with a sincere expression and put a hand to my chest. "I really feel like I forgave him," I said. "I just didn't feel the need to go down there and see him. Is that okay? Does that mean I really haven't forgiven him and I just thought I had? Because I really do feel like I did. I thought about it a lot after I came in here to see you the first time, and I thought I had done a good job of just giving it all to God even though I couldn't understand it."

"What could you not understand?" she asked.

"Why he'd do that. Why something like that would happen to me."

"You may never have a clear answer for that, Claire. You just have to trust that God will be able to use you just like you are—scars and all. It's like the story of the broken pot. You've heard that one, haven't you?"

The first thing that went through my mind when she said broken pot was Humpty Dumpty, but I quickly ruled that out since he was more of an egg—at least he had been in all the illustrations I'd seen. I absentmindedly wondered if anyone really knew what Humpty Dumpty was. *Was he an egg?*

"I take that as a *no*," Ginger said, staring at my blank expression.

"No," I said, "at least I don't think so, unless you're talking about Humpty Dumpty."

She smiled and shook her head.

"Every day, a village woman took two vessels to the well to fill them with water. One of the vessels had a crack, so by the time she made it back to her home, she only had one-and-a-half pots of water. Year after year, this happened until one day, the cracked vessel had enough. He couldn't stand it anymore. *'Hey,'* he said to the lady. *'Why do you continue to use me day after day when I can't even hold my water? Why don't you just get a new pot?'* The woman took the pot into her hands and turned him just the right way so he could see the path she walked along everyday to get to the well. *'See?'* she asked him. *'See all the beautiful flowers along the path?'* The pot looked, and indeed, he saw a colorful array of wildflowers. *'Everyday, I use you to water these flowers,'* she said." Ginger paused and smiled at me. "So every day, without even knowing it, that old, broken pot was being used to grow a beautiful garden."

I reached forward to grab a handful of tissues since tears started welling my eyes.

"We're all broken, Claire. God uses *all* of the events in our lives, the good ones and the bad ones, to mold us into the people we are, and He's able to use us in spite of, and because of our brokenness."

"I'm really not usually this emotional," I said, as I gave another dab to the corners of my eyes.

She smiled as if to say I didn't need to explain such a thing. "And just because you didn't feel the need to go see your uncle on his deathbed doesn't mean you haven't forgiven him. Most people wouldn't even think twice about not going after they'd seen the side of him you did."

"Well, I have forgiven him," I said with quiet confidence since it was something I knew in my heart.

"Did you do your homework?" she asked.

"I did, actually. I got seven of them done on the first day."

"Nice work," she said. "Did they get easier and easier?"

"Not really," I said. "The first one was the easiest, believe it or not."

"The one right out here on the sidewalk?" she asked with a curious expression.

I nodded. "I ran into a childhood friend on the sidewalk, and I told him the whole story about having to hug someone, so he teased me and tickled me into it." I paused, remembering that whole scene a couple of months before.

"What was his name?" she asked.

But because I didn't know she was about to ask a question, I spoke over her, saying, "Wynn's getting married this weekend," at the same time.

We both laughed at how jumbled our words came out sounding.

"Did you say your friend's getting married?" she asked, obviously hearing my statement.

I nodded. "This weekend."

"Is it here in New Orleans?" she asked.

"No. It's in Montana, actually."

"Montana? Is that where his family's from?"

"No. Wynn's dad does business with a man who owns a twelve-bedroom mansion on a lake out near Missoula. It's amazing and picturesque with mountains and everything. I've actually been there once when I went with their family on vacation. Wynn wanted to keep the wedding simple and private, so we're all going up there for the weekend. There's an old chapel in Missoula, so they're gonna have the ceremony there, and we'll all just hang out at the lake house and chill for the weekend."

"Sounds like a fun little holiday," she said.

I shrugged. "I think it's cool that she's so laid back about it. Wynn could have had half of New Orleans at her wedding if she wanted. Her dad has the money to throw whatever party she wanted, and everyone would want to come see her get married, especially now that she's doing so well with her music and everything."

Ginger smiled. "I was gonna ask," she said. "You said her name the last time you were here, and I figured that had to be the same girl. There aren't too many Wynn's. My daughter loves her album, and she's got me listening to it, too. She got it for her birthday."

I smiled. "I'm so proud of her," I said. "It's really amazing how things fell into place with her music. Sometimes I wish I did something where I could directly glorify God with my job like that."

"Broken pot, Claire," she said.

I knew she was right. We all had different jobs to do, and we all had different styles in which we did them.

"So, what was his name?" she asked.

"Who?"

"The young man you felt so comfortable hugging."

"Oh, his name's... his name is Cameron." I had no idea why I said his whole name like that, and I smiled at myself for doing so.

"Cameron?" she repeated in a little bit deeper voice since I said it funny in the first place.

"Cam," I said, giggling at her. "His name's Cam."

"Oh, my word little Miss Claire," she said with wide eyes. "You sure are extra smiley with a side of smiley sauce right now."

I tried to contain my smile by shaking my head, but it was difficult. "I'm just laughing at myself for saying Cameron, that's all. Everyone really only calls him Cam, so it sounded funny."

"He's a handsome young man," she said. I widened my eyes and she motioned to the window. "I didn't spy or anything, but I took a glance when I saw you speaking to him."

"He is handsome," I said. "All-American high-school hero—college hero, too. Heck, life hero. Cam's a golden child."

"Well, like I say, I didn't spy, but I will say, he was smiling at you."

I shook my head at her, feeling unable to stop the huge grin that was spread across my face.

"Have you seen him since you ran into him that day?" she asked.

I shook my head. "No."

"Will he be at this weekend getaway?" she asked.

Again, I smiled uncontrollably as I shook my head at her for putting me on the spot.

"No?" she asked, since I was shaking my head.

"No, it's none of your business," I said, teasing her and making her laugh.

"You like him," she said, with a narrow-eyed expression.

"I do not," I said. "All I said was that I didn't hate hugging him. I don't even think I said that. I think I just said his was my least dreadful of the ten."

"Well, tolerable's a start," she said.

"I hope so."

"It is. And I'm so glad to see you doing so well."

"I didn't know what to think when you told me not to come back," I said.

She smiled. "I knew you'd be back," she said. "At least, I hoped you would. I knew you'd need to process some things."

"I really don't feel like I harbor a grudge with Uncle Todd," I said. "I just wanted to touch base with you about not going to see him when he was dying or whatever. It's not like I dwell on it or anything. I usually just live my life and not even think about it. I just end up getting all emotional when I'm here for some reason."

"Because I know how to ask all the right questions," she said. "Why do you think I keep the tissue, remember?"

54

I smiled at her, and she winked at me. "I'm so glad you came to see me, Claire," she said. Her tone of voice definitely reflected that she thought this might be the last time we saw each other. I wasn't really a therapy type of person, and I had been thinking the same thing—somehow I knew this would be my last appointment with Ginger. I thought it was funny that she knew it, too.

"I'm glad I came to see you, too," I said.

She looked directly into my eyes. "You'll think about all that stuff with your uncle over the years because you're human, and that's what humans do… we think. Just know that none of that was your fault. He should have known better. It shouldn't have happened, but it did, and now we move on. It's a choice we make."

"Yep," I said, since I'd already thought about all that on my own.

She smiled, seeming satisfied with my agreement. "You call me if you have any more questions," she said sincerely. I knew she meant it, but we both knew I wouldn't be back. "You would have been fine without coming to see me, Claire, but I'm so happy you let me be a part of your journey."

I just stared at her, feeling touched by her heartfelt words. I knew she really liked me. "I'm happy I came, too," I said, even though it was a bit awkward for me to stare at someone and say something heartfelt like that. I had to, though.

She smiled and handed me another one of her cards. "Don't lose this," she said. "You'll need my address since I insist on having a Christmas card every year. I'd like it if it was one of the ones with a picture so I can see your family grow."

"What family?" I asked, honestly thinking she was referring to my mom and brother.

She smiled and winked at me like I was being cute, and I took the business card from her as we both stood from our seats. I wasn't sure exactly why I did it... the whole thing sort of just happened without me thinking about it, but as we stood, I initiated a hug. I hugged her. It was a true, unsolicited hug, and Ginger squeezed me back like she was extremely grateful for the gesture. She pinched my cheek and smiled through watering eyes as she pulled back to stare at me.

"I just love you to pieces, Claire King."

"...In the boxing ring," I mumbled under my breath in a silly way.

She gave me a curious expression, and I just smiled.

"Nothin'," I said, shaking my head to answer her unasked question.

She smiled and shrugged it off, before pinching my cheek again. "Bye love," she said.

I smiled and waved as I left her office, feeling encouraged and inspired by the whole bit about the cracked pot. There were all sorts of flowers in the world to be watered, after all.

Chapter 6

A whole crew of us left New Orleans on the same flight, which was bound for Missoula, Montana. We arrived Thursday afternoon. We would have all day Friday to hang out around the house before Wynn and Ryan got married on Saturday. Our flight back was scheduled for Sunday afternoon. It would be a three-night trip, which I knew would pass quickly.

It was literally just family, so there was no rehearsal dinner, or reception, or any other normal wedding things. The chapel, which held about a hundred people, would only be about a quarter full, and that was just the way Wynn wanted it. She and Ryan were both enjoying a little notoriety in their respective professions, and she wanted nothing more than to slip away and enjoy a private ceremony. Her sister had done the same thing when she married Jacob, so I wasn't surprised. I was a little taken aback that she chose Montana, but she said she had fond memories of the vacations they took there. She said she would have just done it in her parent's back yard like Alex did, but she liked the idea of forcing the family into a house for the weekend like the good old days when everyone used to take summer vacations together.

Counting the bride and groom and all the children and babies, there were twenty-three of us traveling together. Ryan's parents came, and so did his older sister who was married with two kids. Ryan also brought his good childhood friend, whose name was Max.

Wynn liked to joke about setting me up with Max so best friends could marry best friends and we could live happily ever after. I'd met him a time or two, and never really taken much interest, but I was curious to see if there was any change since I'd been working through some of my hang-ups. Anyway, Max would be there, but he was the only non-family member Ryan was bringing just like I was the only non-family member Wynn would have there. This was all the more reason she thought it would be cute if we hooked up. She had already mentioned that to me several times.

I liked him and everything, but seeing him there in a side-by-side comparison with Cam was throwing me off. It was funny. If you'd put Max and Cam side by side, you'd definitely say Max was more my style. He was quirky and smaller-framed than Cam. He had a quiet wit that was completely different from Cam's outgoing, life of the party personality. They were total opposites, and on paper, it would look like Max was a sure bet for me.

That wasn't the case, however. I had actually forgotten Max was even coming. Wynn had mentioned it several times, and each time, I never even considered how it would affect me. Cam was different. I never, for a second, forgot that Cam would be there. It was one of the very first things I thought of when Wynn said she wanted to get married in Montana.

There was a resort in Las Vegas called Wynn, and she and Ryan considered flying everyone out to do it there on the sheer principal that it shared her name. Vegas was obviously a top spot for destination weddings, but they decided on the laid-back vibe of Montana, choosing instead to go to Vegas for a couple of nights to kick off their honeymoon (which would eventually take them to France).

It would be easy to be jealous of Wynn.

She had a charmed life.

She was marrying a wonderful guy, and both of them were killing it in their respective careers. I wasn't envious of her, though. I loved her and was thankful for her friendship and for everything the Martins had done for me over the years. She had never begrudged me all those times when her parents paid my way or bought me the same thing they bought her just because I was with them and they didn't want me to feel left out. Wynn was right there, making me feel included. I'd never have ill feelings about whatever level of success Wynn achieved. It was the opposite, in fact. I was really proud of her. She knew that, and she felt the same way toward me, and that's why we'd remained close all these years.

We had a one-hour layover in Denver before catching our final flight into Montana. Cam sat a few rows in front of me on the second flight. I was sitting in the same row with Wynn's little sister, Amelia, and there was an empty chair between us.

The last leg of our flight was only an hour and a half, and we'd been in the air for about thirty minutes when Cam came walking by. I assumed he was walking toward the restroom, and I did my best not to stare at him as he passed. He had on jeans with running shoes and a t-shirt. He was dressed casually, and should not have been making my heart race. I tried to stop myself from glancing at him, but I couldn't manage. I snuck a glance, and was horrified to find that he was looking straight at me as if he was expecting me to look. I instantly glanced down even though I knew I was huge dork for doing so.

Cam only had a few more paces to go before he walked right past me. I didn't look at him again, but as he passed me, he reached out and pinched my arm. I seriously couldn't breathe properly—it was like I'd just been running or something, which I obviously hadn't. I was so relieved that Cam didn't speak to me because I was sure my voice would have come out warbled and breathless. I leaned my head onto the seatback, closing my eyes. I figured if I just took a nap I could avoid any awkward eye contact with people walking down the aisle.

My eyes were still closed two minutes later when I felt a light pinch on my arm, causing me to look up. I was in close proximity with Cam's thigh area, and my eyes instantly shifted further upward to find that he was standing there smiling down at me.

Jitters and jolts of nerves coursed through my body, and I was almost certain that I wouldn't be able to speak if spoken to. *What was wrong with me?* I smiled stiffly, and he lifted his chin like he was motioning for me to do something.

I glanced at Amelia, who was sitting by the window, listening to whatever was coming through her earbuds with her eyes closed. I felt Cam push me by the shoulder when I turned to look at Amelia. I shouldn't say it was a push. It was more of a gentle nudge, but either way it made me turn to look back at him. He lifted his chin again. "Scoot over. I'm going to sit right here for a minute."

"Me?" I asked with a hand to my chest. He smiled and nudged me again, glancing toward his right as if someone might need to get by. I quickly put the tray into its upright position and shifted to the seat next to me. Amelia opened her eyes when she felt the commotion, but she just adjusted so that she was facing the window. I turned just in time to see Cam settle into the seat I had just been sitting in.

"Hey Uncoo Cam," Lane said, peeking his head above the seats in front of us.

"How are you, booger?" Cam asked, reaching out to scratch the little boy's head.

"I'm not a boogoo," Lane said, smiling.

"Okay, you little rascal," Cam said, teasing him.

Lane's face scrunched up like he thought Cam was the silliest thing in the world. "I'm not a wascoo eidoo."

"Okayy," Cam said. "How are you, Lane?"

"Good," the little boy said. "How aww you?"

"I'm good."

"Well," Amelia said from the seat next to me, without looking at them.

Lane turned to stare at her with those precious, curious toddler eyes. "What, Aunt Mewa?"

"Well, punkin," she said sleepily. "You're doing well, not good."

Lane scrunched up his face again, and looked at Cam and me as if asking us to translate what Amelia was saying.

Cam lifted his pinky into the air and made a silly, old man face. "Your Aunt Amelia is speaking of grammar, young chap. Later, she will be retiring to the west wing for tea and crumpets." He spoke with a hilarious imitation of English nobility.

"I'm just teaching him life lessons," she said. She glanced at Lane with a smile and a kiss face before closing her eyes again.

I shifted my gaze back to Cam to see how he would respond. He smiled at Lane. "Aunt Amelia's right about sayin' well, partner, but I like to give her a hard time about going off to college and getting all fancy and educated on us."

"What's a cwumpet?" Lane asked.

"Ask Aunt Amelia," Cam said. "She probably eats them all the time at college."

"What's a cwumpet, Aunt Mewa?" Lane asked.

"It's a cookie," Amelia said sleepily.

I saw Alex talking to Lane from the seat next to him, and within a few seconds, he disappeared. Cam and I turned to face each other, hesitating to say anything for a few seconds as we both wondered if Lane would come popping out from behind the seats again. He didn't, and Cam and I were left staring at each other, both of us smiling. His eyes roamed over my face, and I felt the need to glance away.

"How are you?" he whispered, making me look at him again. I smiled, remembering that whole conversation he just had with Lane.

"Good," I said.

His smiled broadened.

"How are you?" I asked.

"Good," he said. "I haven't seen you in a while." He said that last part like it was something that bugged him, which I couldn't understand because it was nothing for us to go months without seeing each other. In fact, most of the time that was exactly what we did—we'd go months, if not years, without even thinking about it.

"We saw each other not too long ago over by Keller's, remember?"

He let out a little laugh. "Yeah, I remember. That's what I'm talking about. It's been a while since then."

I smiled to myself, thinking, *yeah, and before that it was even longer between times we saw each other*, but I didn't say that.

"Did you manage to give away the rest of those hugs?" he asked.

I glanced at him like I was surprised he remembered so many details of our encounter. "Absolutely," I said. "I did almost all of them that same day."

He scowled at me. "What, did you just walk around town passing them out willy-nilly?"

I smiled and nodded. "You got me goin'," I said with a shrug.

"Did you give them all the stiff-arm?" he asked, holding his arms in front of his chest in a perfect imitation of what I did that day.

I giggled. "No," I said. "You would have been proud. I did it right. I walked right up to them and put my arms around them just like you taught me."

"So, you put your arms right around *Nate Pilgreen*?" he asked, as if he wasn't very fond of the idea.

I giggled again, remembering Nate's look of surprise when I explained to him that I wanted a hug that day. He and I got a good laugh out of that for about the next month, but we had hugged several times since then, all of which were less awkward than the one before it. There was nothing going on between us, but Ginger had been right when she said there was something to human contact, and that it wasn't always perverted.

"I was hoping you still had nine more," Cam said as I was lost in thought. "I was gonna help you out with them on the trip."

My stomach clinched at his words, but I tried to act cool. "Nine more?" I asked in mock disbelief. "You were hoping I *completely failed*?"

"I'd definitely rather you fail than have you huggin' on Nate Pilgreen."

I glanced at the seats in front of us, and then over at Amelia, wondering if anyone could hear us. We were whispering, but I still felt shy about it. Maybe it's because my insides were all torn up with butterflies and nerves, so much that I felt like it was somehow showing physically—emanating from me. *Had Cam just said he had a distaste for me hugging Nate Pilgreen, and if so, what did that mean?*

"You got beef with Nate?" I asked.

"Now I do," he said.

I hesitated for a few seconds, both of us staring at each other.

"What's that mean?" I asked.

More staring.

"It means, now I do," Cam repeated in a quiet tone. He paused and leaned into the aisle, shifting like he was communicating with someone in front of us. He nodded and told the person, "I'm comin'," before looking at me. "I'm helping Cole and them keep Jude occupied," he said as a means of explaining that he had to go.

"Oh, of course," I said.

Cam hesitated for a second like he may say something but then decided against it. He reached out and gave my leg a squeeze before standing up to make his way back up the aisle toward his seat.

Chapter 7

"Admit it, Wynn," Cole said, making us all turn to look at him. He gestured to the board game that was already set up on the table. "You brought us all the way out to Montana just so you could trap us in a house and make us play Cranium."

Everyone looked at Wynn, who smiled and shrugged innocently. "That's a bride's prerogative," she said.

"Amen to that," Debbie (Cole and Cam's mom) said.

"Y'all know how it is," Wynn said. "When we're all at home, we just take off going here and there, and before you know it, we only get to see each other for a few minutes at a time. I wanted us all to be captives for the weekend..." she held up her hands innocently. "...and if a game or two of Cranium gets played in the process..."

"Well I, for one, am excited about it," Debbie said.

"Me too," Kathy agreed.

There were two huge tables sitting side-by-side in the enormous living space. Twelve of us were going to play Cranium, and we gathered around one of the tables, which happened to have the perfect number of chairs. We had already been at the house for a few hours before we decided to play, so everyone had already made introductions with

Ryan's family, some of whom were playing the game with us.

"You might as well not get comfortable," Wynn said, looking around the table before we all sat down. "We're gonna pick teams." We all looked at her, and she smiled. "Okay, it's me, Cole, and Cam as team leaders," she said, pointing at herself and then the both of them. She looked at Ryan, who was sitting next to her. "I got Ryan."

"Why don't we make teams with the people sitting next to us, if you're just gonna pick Ryan?" Cole asked, giving his cousin a hard time. "And who said you get to pick first, anyway?"

Wynn gave Cole a wide-eyed expression that reminded everyone she was the bride. "Who do you want?" she asked.

Cole shrugged and glanced to his right at his wife. "Liv," he said.

"Aww, how cute," Amelia said. "He's gonna pick his wife."

"So did Wynn," Cole said.

"Cam you're next," Wynn said, ignoring all of them.

"Claire," he said without hesitation.

Unlike the rest of them, Cam had not chosen the person who was currently standing next to him. In fact, I was already sitting, and I was right next to Wynn, which was on the complete opposite end of the table from Cam.

Everyone looked at me, and I just smiled, feeling like my heart could go beating right out of my chest.

"*Really?*" Amelia said in an exaggerated annoyed tone, like she was mad at Cam for not choosing her since she was standing right next to him. She quickly smiled, letting us all know she was only joking, and everyone started laughing. Amelia began to move, looking at me like she was ready to give me her seat. I was frozen in place, and I glanced at Cam, wondering what I should do and whether or not my legs would cooperate should I try to walk over there.

Cam smiled and motioned for me to come his way. "Come on," he said. "You're on my team."

"That's good, baby sis, I want you on my team anyway," Wynn said to Amelia. I barely had a chance to stand up before she started patting the seat for her little sister.

I could literally hear the pounding of my own heart in my ears as I walked around the table to take Amelia's spot. I vaguely registered the fact that Cole chose his mom for his team while I was walking toward Cam, who had just sat down. He smiled at me and scooted the chair next to him out so I could sit down. *Bam, bam, bam,* went the pounding of my heart.

There were three teams of four by the time it was all said and done.

Ours consisted of Cam, myself, Ryan's mom, and Ryan's friend, Max.

Ms. Sheila and Mr. Dale (Ryan's parents) were extremely down to earth, and so were his sister, her husband, and Max.

The smack talking was epic. The Martin's were professional smack-talkers. I'd been around them long enough to appreciate their skills tremendously. They made dry-witted remarks referring to their own greatness, but it was obvious that they weren't that full of themselves and they were just doing it for fun. Ryan's family seemed to appreciate the humor in it, and they all laughed a lot at the Martin family banter that was going on between questions and challenges.

We laughed for an hour straight. As soon as we'd stop laughing, someone else would do or say something that would crack us all up again. We laughed so much that it almost felt therapeutic—like something had physically happened to my body from it. I was wondering if it was possible to get a laughing buzz, and thinking about Googling it when Wynn drew the card for our team.

"Okay, y'all have to pick someone to act something out," she said.

"I will," I volunteered, raising my hand a little."

"...And you need somebody to move your body for you," she added.

"Oh," Sheila said, "It's the one where they have to use your arms and act it out for you."

"I'll do it with her," Cam said.

I was so nervous that I honestly felt like my body would give out in someway—either my knees would get wobbly or I would start visibly trembling. I was already delirious from laughing so much, and now Cam was supposed to come stand behind me and use my body as a giant, life-size puppet.

I reached out to take the card from Wynn so I could look at it, and she held it away from me like I was crazy for even trying.

"You can't see," she said. "You have to guess what he's doing."

"I don't get to know?" I asked innocently.

"No," Cam said, reaching in front of me to take the card from Wynn. "Only I get to know. I'm gonna use your arms to act it out, and you get to guess with the rest of the team."

"It's like we did a minute ago with train conductor," Wynn said, reminding me.

"Oh, yeah," I said, nodding.

I stood up and Cam stood behind me. He was close enough that our bodies brushed up against each other. He took my wrists in his grasp, and in one fluid motion he turned us to the side in what was obviously an Egyptian pose. I knew what he was doing within seconds of him starting, but I was too stunned by his touch to make my mouth work.

"Airplane!" Sheila yelled.

"Dancer!" Max said. "Elephant!"

Cam reached up and used his hand to make my head move. He strategically caused my chin to jut in and out in that Egyptian sliding motion before using my hands to do that dance with the crooked up arms again.

It was so obvious that it was an Egyptian.

"Turtle!" Max said.

"Chiropractor!" Sheila yelled.

"Egyptian!" I said, finally.

"Yeah, but a certain one," Cam said, right by my ear.

Max, who had heard him, yelled, "King Tut!"

"Yes!" Cam said, clapping once as he let go of me. He pulled my chair out when I went to sit down, which made me glance around the table to see if anyone had noticed. They hadn't.

"You can't talk," Wynn said, giving Cam a hard time about saying *a certain Egyptian.*

"Oh, come on, they got Egyptian," Cam said.

"Yeah, they got Egyptian," Kathy agreed, nodding.

Cam gave Wynn a shrug as if to say the whole table was on his side, and she stuck her tongue out at him. Everyone laughed as Cole read the next card to Wynn's team.

We stayed downstairs playing Cranium for a another hour or so before some people went to their rooms, leaving seven of us who decided to play Bananagrams for a while.

It was after midnight by the time we all went to bed. I got my own bedroom, which was nice, but at the same time, quiet. My bedroom shared a bathroom with Amelia's, but all I had to do was lock her out if I needed privacy.

I had already showered and had just turned my light off when I heard tapping on my door. "Hello?" I whispered, staring at the door and wondering if I was hearing things. The rooms were big, and there was no way the person on the other side of that door (if there was one) could hear me. I heard the sound of a few more taps followed by the door cracking open.

"Pssstt," I heard Wynn say through the crack.

I smiled. "Come in," I called.

Light from the hallway spilled in behind her. It wasn't very bright out there, but it helped me to see her form as she came inside. She was wearing pajama pants and a T-shirt. We basically looked like twins.

"Are you cold?" She asked, plopping on the end of my bed.

I had just cuddled up in a fluffy comforter and was feeling utterly blissful. "No way," I said. "It's warm under here."

Wynn slapped her hands onto the bed and stared at me with eyes that grew as big as saucers. It was pretty dark in there, but the door was open, and my eyes had adjusted enough that I could see her face. I giggled at her googly-eyed expression.

"What in the world was going on down there?" she asked, staring at me with great intensity.

I giggled at the sheer drama. "What do you mean?" I asked.

"Y'all's chemistry was crazy down there!" she said.

I could feel blood rushing to my cheeks, and I was thankful for the darkness. I made a tiny squealing noise, scrunching up my face.

"I had no idea you and Max would hit it off," she continued. "I can't believe it how much y'all like each other."

My face fell and I stared at her, wondering if she could possibly be serious. "Max?" I asked.

She stared at me for several long seconds before she could no longer hold a straight face. She leaned over, in a silent belly-laugh that had me scowling trying to make sense of it all. "Oh my gosh, no, not *Max*," she said, shaking her head. "Cam, Cam, Cam, obviously. What in the world, Claire? Y'all were looking at each other like two lovebirds sitting in a tree! And then he got up behind you like that, moving your arms around."

"Lots of people had to do that," I said. "That was part of the game."

"Yeah, but Cam was sweet on you when he did it."

I covered my face with my hands and giggled a little. "No he wasn't," I said. "I don't even know what that means."

"It means, what in the world is going on with you and my cousin?" she said.

"Nothing!" I insisted, still whispering.

"That's not what I saw," she said. She stared at me intently in the near darkness. "Claire, you know something was going on. Don't lie."

"I'm not. It's nothing. I ran into him on the sidewalk a couple months ago, and we haven't seen each other since."

"Why'd he pick you first?" she asked.

I shrugged. "I guess to annoy Amelia."

She shook her head. "I'm not buying it," she said. "Something's going on."

"Nothing's going on," I promised.

"Do you *like* him?" she asked.

"Nooo," I said, mostly for her sake since I felt like it might be weird for her to think about me flirting with her cousin.

"Well, I think he likes *you*," she said.

I shook my head and smiled like she was out of her mind.

"What if you really married my cousin?" she asked dreamily. "You'd be a Martin!"

That statement made my heart skip a beat, but I tried to stay collected. "In two days, you'll be a Collins," I said, shifting the topic to her upcoming marriage since talking about Cam caused brain fog and speechlessness.

"Can you believe it?" she asked.

"No," I said. I put my hand on hers, and she returned my touch, holding my hands.

"I love you Clairebear," she said. "I'm so glad you're here."

"I love you, and I'm glad, too," I said. "I think you and Ryan are perfect."

"Thank you," she said, letting my hand go so she could stand up. "I keep feeling like I need to pinch myself." She stood beside my bed like she was about to leave, and I sat up. She reached out to pinch my hand. "Night," she said.

"Night."

"I'm okay with you liking my cousin," she said. It seemed like she hesitated to say it at first, and then she decided to go ahead, looking and sounding uncertain the whole time she spoke. "I know you said you don't like him or whatever, but I wanted you to know that I would be okay with it if you did. You know, just in case you were saying that because you thought I'd care."

"I wasn't saying it just for you," I said. "There's nothing going on with me and Cam."

"Okayyy," she said. "But I was just saying that if you ever thought about it or whatever and it crossed your mind to wonder how I felt about it, then I think it's wonderful. I would love to see you with Cam. I think you two would be perfect for each other—probably more perfect than either of you even know."

"Oh my gosh, Wynn, stop," I said.

"Okay, I won't butt-in," she said with her hands raised.

"It's not happening," I said.

"Okay," she said innocently as she turned to walk out.

"Love you," I called.

"Love you, too," she said.

"See you in the marnin," I added, being silly.

"They got that fancy espresso maker down there," she said.

"Y'all need to wait for me to work that," I said.

"You better get your butt up early," she said.

"Never mind, y'all just go ahead and burn y'allselves if y'all need y'all's coffee that early." I said, wearing out the word y'all and making her giggle as she walked out the door.

Chapter 8

Wynn and Ryan were to be married Saturday at 2PM, which meant we had all day Friday to hang out and check out Missoula. The weather was perfect, so about half of us went for a hike at a nearby state park while the others went shopping.

The shoppers found out about a small festival that was happening downtown. Apparently, it was to start Friday afternoon and go through Sunday. I wasn't with the ones who got the details, but they said there would be music, food, and crafts.

We all went to it Friday evening—every single one of us, babies and all. It was a thirty-minute drive, but we were glad we ventured out, because the little "festival" had a really cool vibe. I wasn't quite old enough to appreciate Missoula fully the last time I was there, so I was a bit surprised by how charming it was.

We drove the four rental SUV's, and parked as close to each other as we could manage. I pretty much stuck by Wynn, since that was par for the course with us. I saw Cam take note of me when we got in the trucks to drive over there. He was driving one of them, and it happened to not be the one I got into. I didn't do that intentionally, but I couldn't help but notice Cam take note of it.

"I think we should stick to small groups and stay in touch with phones," Wynn said, taking charge as we all congregated on the sidewalk near the parking lot where we all found a spot.

"Cam promised Jude some ice cream," Cole said. "So that'll be our first stop."

Everyone started stating what their plans were, and we all just sort of dispersed, agreeing to stay in groups and keep in touch. I went with Wynn, Ryan, Sheila, Dale, and Max. Sheila and Dale got sidetracked by a booth that was selling local honey and bee pollen, and she tugged him in that direction, leaving me with Wynn, Ryan, and Max. After the conversation I had the night before with Wynn, I figured she knew I wasn't interested in him, and that seemed to be the case because she completely stopped dropping hints about it or encouraging it in any way.

We ate dinner at the festival, which had tons of food options. I chose the Pad Thai from a noodle booth because it had the longest line. I'd seen other people eating it, and it looked good. I wanted to try one of everything, but at the same time, I wasn't hungry at all. Nerves would do that to a person. I knew I shouldn't be anxious about running into Cam, but I couldn't help it. I kept thinking he'd be around every corner. The Pad Thai was delicious, but I only ate about eight bites of it before throwing it away. I did, however, get a fresh-squeezed strawberry lemonade from a different booth, and had no problem finishing that.

Wynn had posted a picture of us on her social media, and someone working at the festival caught wind of her presence. While we were eating, the festival director approached her, asking if she wouldn't mind singing a song on one of the little side stages before she left. As her best friend, I knew she did not want to do it. She loved performing, but I knew she was in the mood to fade into the background that day. No one besides those of us closest to Wynn knew that was the case, though, because she smiled and agreed to do it easily. The guy was so appreciative that he handed her an envelope with two hundred "festival-dollars" to be spent on food or art.

Wynn turned around and handed it to me the second it was in her possession. "For that kaleidoscope you liked."

"I'm so sure," I said, pushing it away with a grimace. "That's yours."

"It's yours, but you're not getting it for free." Wynn paused and looked at the director. "We'll need two mics and an acoustic guitar. My friend will be singing harmony."

He smiled and shrugged. "Sounds like a plan to me," he said. "Two for the price of one."

"I couldn't—" I said, knowing we hadn't practiced anything together in months.

Wynn looked at me with a pleading expression that only I could see. "Please," she whispered. I could tell she meant it, so I agreed.

The guy told us a time and place and walked away grinning from ear to ear. I was so nervous that I felt sick. "Why are we doing this?" I asked, handing her the envelope that I'd been numbly holding while the guy was there.

"Keep it," she said, pushing it back at me. "It's perfect to get you your toy. You can get the best one with that."

I really did want that kaleidoscope, and I smiled as I stashed the envelope in my purse. "Thank you!" I said.

"Seriously," she said. "Thank you. I really didn't feel up to doing it, and having you up there with me takes so much of the pressure off."

"You didn't have to agree," Ms. Kathy said, taking up for her daughter.

"It's fine, Mom. He was nice, and I'm okay doing it."

"I think it's a compliment that he was so excited about it," Sheila said, chiming in proudly. "I can't believe two-hundred-whole-dollars for one song. I can't wait to hear y'all."

"You wanna just do Summertime?" I asked since we'd sung it together many times before.

"That's great," she said. "I was gonna say, "Feelin Good, but I know Summertime better on guitar. That's perfect." She leaned over and put a hand on my leg. "Seriously, chica, thanks for doing this with me."

We did it. It all sort of passed in a blur, but we went to the stage, the guy announced us, the crowd cheered, and Wynn said a few words about being happy to be there on such a gorgeous evening. The small but sweet crowd responded to us warmly. She engaged me, and I spoke into my mic, feeling the whole time like I was dreaming. Wynn sat with the guitar propped on her knee, and I stood, holding the mic in my hand instead of putting it on a stand.

We sang together like we had done so many times in the past, and when we were done, everyone who'd been listening got to their feet. We both bowed, and Wynn blew kisses before we made our way back to the area where our family was standing.

Wynn's sister was standing there with Lane on her hip, and he wiggled till she let him down so he could run over to Wynn. The festival director was just walking up to say something to us when he ran into her arms.

"Is this your little boy?" he asked Wynn.

"No sir, he's my sister's."

He stuck his finger out in Lane's direction the way people do with babies. "What's your name?" he said, smiling and looking straight at Lane.

"Wane," Lane said.

"Hello, Wayne!" the guy said, smiling. "How are you?"

"I'm Wane," Lane said a little louder.

"Lane," Alex said.

"Oh, Laaane," he said, making Lane smile and nod.

"Listen, I just wanted to thank you again," he said, looking at Wynn. He smiled and shifted to look at me. "You too, that was just beautiful. Thank you ladies so much."

"You're welcome," we both said at the same time.

He was so sweet that I was glad we did it. I smiled as he walked away, remembering the way he confidently called Lane Wayne.

"I think you should go over there right now," Wynn said. She regarded me with an intense stare that made me give her a worried expression.

"Where?" I asked, looking over my shoulder.

"Over there by those crafts," she said, turning me by the shoulders. "Just trust me and walk over there. Act like you're getting me a lemonade."

I started walking toward the lemonade stand, and within seconds, I could see why Wynn felt the need to send me in that direction. Cam was standing there, talking to his dad. He glanced at me as I approached, but there was basically nothing I could do. I wasn't going to walk right up to them and randomly strike up a conversation, so I just proceeded to the lemonade stand as planned. Mr. Steve noticed Cam looking at me, and he glanced my way. I smiled at both of them from about ten feet away as I headed to get lemonade.

Did I already mention that this lemonade stand came with it's own strong man? I don't believe I did, and it's definitely worth noting, that at this particular festival, the lemonade was fresh squeezed by a big, hunky, beefcake of a guy. It was part of the shtick, for sure. He must have been the owner, actually because his face and muscle-bound image was part of the logo on the cup. A girl with an apron took your money and then the body builder went to work squeezing your lemons. It was tasty lemonade, and the whole tough-guy thing made it an entertaining experience. I was happy to get another cup of it. I stood, staring at the lemon-squeezing man while I waited my turn. I couldn't help but notice that he also happened to be handsome in the face. The whole thing had a hunky fireman vibe that was somehow hilarious and perfect for lemonade.

"Ma'am this is your third one tonight," Cam said, coming to stand right beside me in line. "We're gonna have to ask you to lay off the lemonade."

"Second," I said.

Cam's face fell. "Seriously, it's your second? I was kidding about you coming multiple times. I was saying you were coming for..." he trailed off, gesturing to the hunk, and I smiled.

"I was," I said. "I am." I gestured at the guy with a completely straight face." I don't really even want the lemonade," I said. "I just used that as an excuse to come over here."

It was the truth; I just didn't add that I wanted to see Cam and not the lemonade guy.

"I saw you sing with my cousin," he said.

"One strawberry lemonade," I said since the lady was waiting for my order. I gave her my money and Cam and I stepped aside to watch the squeezing of the lemons. "I've sang with your cousin lots of times," I said, getting back to his statement.

"I know, but I've never..." Cam hesitated. "I think it's been a long time since..." he hesitated again. "I don't know. It sounded really good, that's all. You sounded good. You have such a sweet..." He hesitated again, shaking his head.

"Thank you," I said. I was saying it to Cam, but it also worked for the guy who handed me my lemonade.

Cam and I stood off to the side so we wouldn't be right in the way of other people. "I'm gonna head over here," I said with a flick of my head toward the guy who made kaleidoscopes.

"I'll go with you," Cam said.

"You don't know where I'm going."

"It doesn't matter," he said. "But we better make it quick. It looks like everyone's sort of meeting up." He motioned the area where the rest of the family was now congregating.

"Wynn wants to get back, I'm sure, but she knows I'm going to get this before we leave," I said. "They'll wait for us."

"I have the keys to one of the Tahoes, anyway" Cam said, shaking his front pocket. "Maybe we should just let them leave."

Cam walked with me to the booth where an older gentleman was selling beautiful, handmade kaleidoscopes. I knew right where his booth was and exactly the one I wanted to buy when I got there, so it only took a couple of minutes for me to complete the transaction.

We all piled into the same vehicles we rode in on the way there, so I was not with Cam, and we both seemed a little bummed about it. Someone in my truck had to stop at a drugstore on our way back to the house, which meant everyone else was already home by the time we got there.

The kaleidoscope was a hit, though, and it kept us occupied while we were on the road. I was thrilled to have it. I had seen something similar to it when I was a child, and I thought it would be the coolest thing in the world to own one. I wanted to make sure I got it home safely, so the first thing I did when we got back to the house was bring it to my room and set it on the dresser. I was only up there for a minute before heading back downstairs to hang out with everyone.

Wynn had some other game she wanted us to play. Most everyone else complained about her making us play games, but we secretly loved it and made our best memories while we were being big idiots together. We played one with headbands and another one that involved drawing and was similar to Pictionary. Everyone teased me for being overqualified since I was the resident cartoonist. They said I had to draw left hand, and we had a good laugh about that. They went on and on about my skills while we were playing, and my team completely obliterated the competition, which was a fun way to end the evening. I caught myself feeling grateful to be a part of such a nice family, even if it was by adoption.

It was after midnight when we all went to our rooms, and even then, Wynn feared that we were wasting valuable family time by going to bed so early. Ryan had to remind her she needed to save some energy for getting married the next day.

We went to bed laughing. We'd been laughing so much on this trip that my face was literally sore. I wouldn't have noticed it, actually, but after Max mentioned his cheeks were hurting from laughing, I realized that mine were, too. So did everyone else. We collectively had sore cheeks, and we laughed about that as well, which was extra funny and ironic.

We were all delirious by the time we went to bed. I had just pulled the covers over me when I heard tapping at my door the same as the night before. Cam and I had several moments of extended eye contact when we were playing the drawing game, and I figured Wynn was coming to tease me about it. I sat up, smiling and waiting for her to come in like she did the night before.

The door never opened; instead, there was another tap—three or four of them actually. "Psssttt," I said, from the bed, telling her to come in.

There was more tapping.

I got up and crossed to the door once I realized that Wynn wasn't coming in. I thought maybe she had tried to but I had accidently locked it.

I opened it to find Cam standing there. I was so totally expecting Wynn that I said, "Why didn't you just come in?" as I opened the door.

"Because I didn't want to walk in on you changing," Cam said as if stating the obvious.

My gaze drifted upward to meet his. "I thought you were Wynn," I whispered.

"I'm Cam," he said with a straight face.

I smiled. "I know."

I peered, over his shoulder, behind him, and down the long hallway that led to the stairs before pulling back to meet his gaze again.

"What's up?" I asked.

Chapter 9

"Claire," Cam said, staring at my face like he was slightly confused by his inability to stop staring at me.

"Cam, what?" I asked moving my face out of his line of vision so he would snap out of it.

He blinked at me, tilting his head. "I want to know you," he said finally, but he said it in such a way that it seemed like he was settling for it when he actually wanted to say something else. I could see by his thoughtful expression that he was trying to choose his words carefully.

I took a step back, feeling stunned by his sincerity. I wasn't used to seeing Cam like this, and it had me feeling all gooey inside. "You *do* know me, Cam. You've been knowing me ever since we were kids."

"Not like that," he said, causing little waves of anticipation to course through me.

I didn't know what to say, so I just opened the door to let him come in. Enough light spilled into the room that I easily crossed to the bedside stand and turned on the lamp without having to feel around. He was standing near the door wearing plaid pajama pants and a grey tank top that fit him tightly, like more of an undershirt. Technically, it was a shirt, but I could see every curve of his chest. He knew what he was doing to me by coming in here like that. He knew what he looked like. I did my best not to stare, but it was difficult.

I motioned for him to follow me to the far side of the room and began digging through the heavy curtains to find the sliding glass door that was on the other side.

Every room in the house boasted it's own private balcony. I had been on the main deck quite a bit with the others, but I hadn't yet been on mine, so I fumbled with the lock. Cam smiled and reached out to take over, making quick work of unlocking and opening the door. He held it open just the right way where his arm was above me in an arch as I stepped outside. I passed underneath it glancing up at him with a smile.

There were two Adirondack chairs over toward the right, but I didn't feel like sitting. I walked out to the rail before I turned around so I could lean on it. I heard Cam closing the glass door, and by the time I faced him, he was already headed toward me. He stood next to me, putting his hands on the rail and looking out at the mountains. It was dark out, but it was a clear night, and the moon and stars were bright enough for us to see the shapes of the beautiful, mountainous countryside.

I turned so I could stare out with him. "Big sky country," I said, because I was too nervous to think of anything better.

He smelled and looked like he had just taken a shower. His hair, which had gotten longer on top, was combed away from his face. I looked at his profile and actually had the thought that he might be the world's most perfect-looking man. He had a classic nose and jaw structure with the ideal amount of facial hair peppering the edges. His dark eyes and eyelashes were what put it over the top. Suddenly, he turned to look at me. He was wearing an expression like he was waiting for me to say something.

"What?" I asked, vaguely registering that he had just asked me a question while I was busy staring at him. He smiled as if he was amused by the fact that I was such a space case.

"I said tell me something I don't know about you, Claire King."

"I did not hear you say that at all," I said.

He smiled. "I know. You were in no man's land."

"I don't have a middle name," I said. "That's something you might not know about me."

"You don't have one at all?"

I smiled and shrugged. "My mom just said she couldn't think of anything that sounded good in between Claire and King so she left it blank." I paused and gave him a little smirk. "Also, she made up King. She never really liked her own last name, and I guess she didn't want to name me after the guy, you know, my dad, or whatever. I think his last name was Cobblestone or something."

"Cobblestone?" Cam asked.

I let out a little laugh and shrugged. "Probably not, but I think it started with a C. I saw her write it one time when I was little, and I tried not to get a good look at it because I didn't really want to know. King's fine with me."

"King's a good last name," Cam said. "I can't believe your mom just made it up, though. I didn't even know you could do that."

I giggled. "I guess you can call a baby just about anything you want," I said.

He let out a laugh. "I saw this YouTube video about baby names the state office rejected. You wouldn't believe some of the things parents tried to name their babies."

"I'm pretty glad she went with Claire King, I guess."

"I think I've only met your mom a couple of times," Cam said. I could tell he was doing his best to remember. "She might have come to a carwash we were having in middle school."

"It's probably been a while," I said.

"And your dad was never around," he added thoughtfully.

"Nope," I said. "I'm half errfan. That's probably why I was always tryin' to tag along witchy'all."

I mispronounced the word orphan, and said the whole thing in a silly way since I didn't want to get too heavy.

"What's errfan?" he said.

I laughed. "Orphan," I said. "But I was just messing around, anyway. I have a mama."

Cam moved to stand behind me. It happened so quickly that I didn't realize what he was doing. I felt nervous and jumpy, and I turned in his grasp, pulling back a little. "Careful," he said, putting a hand behind my back to protect me from getting too close to the edge even though I was in no real danger.

"Where are you going?" I asked, bobbing a little like I was anticipating his next move.

"Claire, just relax for a second." He took me by the arm, and pulled me toward him. In one motion, he positioned me in front of his chest. He crossed my own arms in front of my chest in my most-preferred position before wrapping his own arms around me.

He held me securely in place as we faced the mountains. It was a cool evening—much cooler than it was in Louisiana this time of year, and I shivered, shrinking even more deeply into his arms. We stayed like that for several long seconds with my heart beating like crazy. I was terrified and overjoyed at the same time.

"You must be cold," I said since small talk was all I could come up with at the moment.

"Not really," he said, acting comfortable and confident. "It's in the sixties."

"Yeah, but I'm shivering," I said.

He held me there for a few more seconds before he spoke again. "That's not from being cold," he said, finally. He was absolutely right, which only made my case of the shivers worse. I giggled and started to wiggle in his arms, but he ran his hands along my upper arms in an effort to warm me up. I loved the caring way in which he held me. There was no pressure at all. It was as if he was just doing it to make sure I was warm. I never would have expected this type of tender affection from a guy like Cam, and I felt dizzy and confused by it. If there was such a thing as a love bug, I reckoned I'd been bit by it.

"What about you?" I asked, trying to keep my cool.

"What about me?"

"Tell me something I don't know," I said.

I cringed after I said it, hoping he wouldn't tell me something about Jolene—or even anything from the whole era of Jolene. Cam was quiet for several seconds.

"I'm learning how to speak Japanese. I've been taking classes for almost two years."

"That's awesome! Really?" I asked.

He nodded. "That's not really the part of it that I'm telling you about," he said. I shifted to stare at him with a curious expression and he smiled down at me, shrugging me into position where I stood up against his chest again. "My brother has no idea. Nobody does. That's how competitive we are. I know we'll be going to Japan for a store opening in a few months. I've been studying the language ever since I first heard we were looking at a couple of international sites." He paused, and I felt his chest shaking with laughter. "I'm pretty fluent by now," he said. "I can't wait to see his face when we get there."

I turned in his grasp and pulled back so I could stare at him. "You learned a whole other language so you could see the *look on your brother's face*."

"Yes," he said with an easy grin. He shrugged. "I mean, I've always wanted to learn another language anyway. It's just a bonus to freak Cole out a little bit. He'll probably have Rosetta Stone downloaded by the time we get back to the states."

I laughed, remembering all the competitive shenanigans that happened over the years with the Martin boys.

"Say something," I said, shifting to stare at him with a look of challenge.

Cam knew what I was asking him to do, and the next thing I knew, a long stream of Asian-sounding words came out of his mouth. He had the fluctuation and the accent and everything.

I couldn't help but giggle at how good he was. "That was amazing!" I said. "Were you born in Japan or something?"

He smiled.

"Cole's gonna freak out," I said. "When are y'all going?"

"This fall," he said.

"What'd you say?" I asked.

"I said later this fall," he repeated.

"No, what'd you say in Japanese just now," I asked.

He tilted his head, deciding how he wanted to respond. "Actually, I said some things you don't need to know about," he said in a dry tone.

I narrowed my eyes. "Like what?"

He smiled. "I said some nice things about you," he said. "But that's all I'm saying."

A hot, rushing sensation flowed through my body at the way he was looking at me. I swallowed hard. "Cam, I'm not, I, uh…" I fumbled over my words as I stared up at him.

He used his fingertip to trace my eyebrow and down onto my cheek, looking at me like he was examining my every feature.

"Cam," I said pulling away.

His eyes met mine. "I would never hurt you, Claire," he said, barely touching the side of my face with his palm.

"I know you wouldn't," I said like that was the last thing on my mind.

He leaned over to make me look at him. "I feel like you needed to know that, though. I won't hurt you."

"I know you won't," I said, shaking my head and taking a step back.

"Because you won't give me the opportunity to," he said, seeing me pull away.

I shook my head. "Stop, Cam, I don't even know what you're talking about."

"I'm talking about the fact that you want to kiss me and I want to kiss you, and you're not gonna let it happen because you're too afraid I'll hurt you." He paused, but then added, "What I'm telling you is that I won't."

"It's not really like that," I said, shaking my head shyly.

"What's it like?" he asked, "Because it's certainly not as straightforward as, *I like you, you like me, let's make this happen.*"

"Well, of course it's not, Cam. We've known each other for years, and we've never once had a *let's make this happen* moment between us."

"Why not?" he asked as if he was genuinely puzzled.

I smiled. "Because, Cam, we're different. You're a jock and I'm a nerd, and we—"

"You're not a nerd," he said, interrupting me in mid-sentence. "Don't be ridiculous."

"You know what I mean," I said. "One of these things is not like the other. I'm not a Jolene."

There it was.

I said it.

Even in my own thoughts, I'd been trying to avoid that name, but it just popped out of my mouth.

He pulled back a little when I said it, creating some distance between us. "So you think that Jolene, or girls like her, are basically the female version of me, therefore that's the type of woman I should be stuck with."

"I didn't say any of that, and I certainly wouldn't call it being *stuck* with someone like Jolene. She was Miss Louisiana, Cam."

"You think I don't know she was Miss Louisiana, Claire? I only heard that fact about *seven thousand times* over the last few years. I *don't care* that she was Miss Louisiana. That was a long time ago, and it means nothing to me."

I sighed, but before I could speak he said, "Do you really think I'm that shallow?"

We both stared, each of us searching the other's eyes for questions that neither of us asked.

"I definitely don't think you're shallow," I said. I'd been around the Martins long enough to know what kind, sincere, anti-shallow people they were. "I guess I'm just a little confused about what's going on here," I said, feeling shaky and vulnerable.

Cam grinned and lifted one shoulder. "I'm confused, too, if it makes you feel any better."

Chapter 10

"Stay right here," I said with a little squeeze to his forearms, which were gloriously wrapped around my middle. I tiptoed inside to get the plush throw blanket from off the foot of my bed. I remembered thinking how cozy it would feel to go out on the balcony while I was wrapped up in it, and I seized the opportunity to make it happen.

I crossed to the foot of the bed where I picked up the super-soft blanket, turning it over my arm to carry it outside. I had just begun to head back to the balcony when I heard a *tap, tap, tap* on my door. I turned to see that it was still cracked open from when Cam had come in.

"Pssstt," Wynn said, peeking inside.

I saw her shadow moving as she came in, and I instinctually sat on the edge of the bed with the blanket on my lap, acting as casual as possible. I was sitting there when she came in. It was a bit of an awkward pose, sitting at the end of the bed with nothing but a blanket on my lap, but I smiled at her. I could see her wide-eyed expression even in the near-darkness.

"What in the world was goin' on with you guys down there? she asked, crossing over to me in an excited, hunched-over pose.

"Who?" I asked.

"You and Cam!" she whispered, looking at me like I was crazy for asking such a thing as she sat beside me on the bed. It didn't hit her until after she had already sat down beside me that it was odd for me to be sitting there like that.

She pulled back and looked me over. "What are you doing?"

I leaned back on my hand casually like I'd totally been hanging out on the end of the bed intentionally.

"Were you just sitting here?" she asked, glancing down at the blanket for a Kindle, or a phone, or anything that would explain my odd seat choice.

"No," I said. "I was just getting this blanket. I was cold."

"Oh," she said, easily as if that was all the explanation she needed.

She sat back on her hand and smiled at me like she was ready to have a slumber party—like she was prepared to stay there all night. This could obviously not happen since *Cam was on the balcony!*

"Where's Ryan?" I asked, glancing nervously at the door.

"In his room," she said. She put a hand on my leg and gave it a shake. "What's going on with you and my cousinnnn?" she asked with huge, comically intense eyes.

"Nothing," I whispered.

"Yes there is," she said, scowling at me and making me smile. "For reals, Clairebear, you can't trick me. I've never seen you act that way toward him, or him act that way toward you." She pushed at my leg again, trying to get me to admit it.

It was at that very second that Cam started opening the glass door. The curtain was blocking them from seeing each other, but I knew it would only be a matter of seconds before he busted into the room. I was so nervous that it felt a bit like my heart leapt out of my chest.

"Whoa," I said, standing up, and trying to make a last ditch effort at a distraction. "Whoa, whoa," I said. I began bobbing to and fro as if I was really off balance. I wobbled in a semi-circle around the foot of the bed, so that Wynn's back would be facing the door that Cam was about to walk through. "Whoooa," I said again, still acting like a big, wobbling dork.

"What, Claire?" Wynn asked with a concerned expression. "What is it? Are you okay?"

I glanced for the briefest of seconds over her shoulder, but every second seemed like an hour, and it felt like it was taking forever for Cam to come inside. I cleared my throat to mask the sound of the door closing. "Whoa, I got a little dizzy there," I said, shaking my head.

"I saw that," she said.

And because I'm a huge, gigantic goober who cannot contain my own nervous laughter, I began giggling. I shook my head, trying to stop myself, but it was useless. I giggled for several seconds before I could get control of myself and stop.

"What in the world is wrong with you?" she asked.

I shook my head and looked directly at her, still feeling teary-eyed from laughing. Cam was standing behind her by that point, but I didn't dare break eye contact with her to focus on him. Out of my periphery, I watched him put his hands into the air as if to tell me he wasn't sure what to do next. My eyes widened slightly as I tried to convey a silent message to him to *please remain quiet.*

"Claire, you are freaking me out," Wynn said, assuming my wide-eyed expression was aimed at her.

"This is not what it looks like," I said.

"What's not what it—" she cut off short of finishing her question because while she was asking it, she turned to scan the room. "What, what in the… Cam. What are you…" She turned to look at me. "Cam," she said with a serious, wide-eyed expression that only I could see. She pointed at him from in front of her shoulder where he couldn't see. "That's my cousin," she whispered.

I nodded.

"Did he just come out of those curtains?" she whispered, looking a bit stunned.

"He did, but that's because we were standing outside. We weren't… It's not what you think."

"It's definitely not what you think," Cam agreed easily as he walked toward us. He looked at Wynn.

"Wait, what do you think?" he asked. "Because it might be what you think."

"We were just standing out there taking in the view, or whatever," I said.

Wynn crossed to her cousin and reached up to kiss him on the cheek. "I don't want to crash the party," she said. "I came by to tell Claire goodnight, but I was just leaving." She came to the place I was standing near the foot of the bed to hug me.

"You don't have to go," I said, because I was nervous.

"Oh, you want me to stay and hang out witchy'all?" Wynn asked, teasing us.

"Yes," I answered, bluffing.

"No," Cam said. "I want you to get ya 'lil butt los so I can pass some time wit Ms. Claire over here." Cam was great at a Cajun accent, and for that last statement, he turned it on in the most charming way possible.

It was so sweet that Wynn covered her face and let out a squeal. "Did you just say you wanted to *pass some time* with Claire?" she asked, latching on to my arm like we were the pink ladies or something.

Cam smiled. "Yeah, and I said I wantchu tuh get cha 'lil butt los, too."

She squealed again, and then she kissed me on the cheek. "I'm leavin', she said. "Night."

"You're getting married tomorrow," I reminded her.

"I know," she said, smiling and raising her eyebrows.

I gestured to Cam with a flick of my head in his direction. "I'll kick him out if you wanna hang out and get pumped about your big day."

She scoffed at me. "No way," she said. "I wasn't planning on staying even when I didn't know you had a stowaway."

My stomach was full of butterflies. I felt like I was in high school, getting caught kissing under the bleachers. Having that thought made me almost come out and tell Wynn we hadn't been kissing, but I knew that'd just make us seem guiltier than we were. I sighed and smiled, trying to keep myself from over-talking.

"Y'all be good," Wynn said, winking from over her shoulder as she walked out.

"We are being good," I whispered as she walked out and closed the door.

As soon as it was closed, my head whipped around and I stared at Cam with a silly, wild-eyed expression, freaking out that we'd been caught.

He just shrugged with his palms up as if to say he had no idea Wynn was there when he came in.

"We weren't even *doing anything* and we got caught," I said, shaking my head. "Now she's gonna think something happened."

"What's so bad about that?" Cam asked.

I walked slowly toward him, not really knowing whether or not we'd go back outside or what we would do from there. I thought his question was rhetorical, so I didn't answer it. Cam reached out to take the blanket out of my hands, and since I was basically in the twilight zone from being caught, I easily let go of it.

"Come on," he said, laughing at me. He held the blanket in one hand and reached out to take my hand with the other, pulling me outside.

"What are we doing?" I asked, with highly doubtful undertones.

Cam stopped walking just before we got to the door. He was about to reach out to move the curtain, but before he did, he leveled me with a sincere stare. I stared back at him, wondering why he was being so serious.

"I don't want to stay if you're not into it. Just tell me if you want me to go. It's not a big deal." He said it with a little non-committal half-smile that let me know he wouldn't have his feelings hurt if I needed to kick him out.

I'd been making it by on this push-pull thing I had going on, but now he was standing there asking me to say where I stood one way or the other—to tell him whether to stay or go. I hesitated for long enough that he must have thought I wanted him to leave. He tried to hide his disappointment as he grinned. He started to hand me the blanket.

"It's all good," he said. "I'm tired anyway."

I shook my head at his offer to hand me the blanket and leave. He nudged the blanket into my hands as he leaned forward. I had no idea what he was doing at first, but I realized he was placing a kiss on my cheek.

"Night," he said just before he put a quick kiss on the top part of my cheek near the corner of my eye. The idea of Cam Martin's mouth on me seemed utterly fantastical—like something that would only happen in a movie. I honestly didn't know what to do with myself. I could barely breathe.

"Stay," I squeaked out before he could pull back all the way.

"What?" he asked, even though I was pretty sure he heard me.

"Stay." I repeated. "I'm not tired yet."

He opened the curtains, and I reached for the door, and before I knew it, we were standing on the balcony again. Cam opened the blanket, draping it over his shoulders and down his arms like two huge wings. He stepped behind me and wrapped me up, causing me to giggle and squeal a little at my new cocoon. I quickly stopped, however, because I didn't want him to let me go.

I settled into his arms, looking out at the breathtaking scenery. The temperature was perfectly cool and I was now wrapped in a cozy shell with the one and only Cam Martin. It was seriously like a scene from a movie with all the stars and the lake and the moon. And Cam. What was there to say about Cam, but wow—just wow. I never before dared to entertain thoughts of a romantic encounter with either of the Martin boys, let alone Cam. He was Mister New Orleans, and I was... well, I was Claire.

The level of butterflies I was experiencing was astounding. I had never let myself consider the possibility of being with Cam, and now that I was giving into it, twenty years of butterflies got unleashed all at once. I was so crazy about him that I felt like my body was vibrating. He held me close but still with great gentleness as if letting me know I could step out of his grasp any time. I turned my head to the side and leaned into him, trying to convey that I didn't want to go anywhere.

"We've got to do something about it," he said after a few minutes of us just standing there, breathing. (Or in my case, barely breathing.)

"About what?" I asked.

"About Wynn thinking something was going on."

I shrugged because I trusted Wynn and I knew it was no big deal.

"I think we should do something," he said.

I shook my head, still staring at the mountains and enjoying the feel of his arms and the blanket around me. "Do something about what?" I asked.

"About everyone assuming I kissed you while we were out here."

A warm, stabbing sensation hit my gut at his words, and I physically leaned forward an inch or two, shaking my head to detract from my movement.

"No one said everyone assumed that," I said, pretending to be coy.

"They do," Cam said, nodding dryly. "They all think we're kissing up a storm out here."

"Up a storm, huh?" I asked. My head was nestled next to his jaw and neck, so he couldn't see me, but there was obviously a smile in my voice.

"Yep, they're all talking about it like crazy in there," he added in that same dry tone as if he was completely serious.

"Whatta we do?" I asked. I was short of breath as I waited for his answer.

"We confirm the rumors, of course," he said.

"And we do that by—"

"Kissing," he said in a matter of fact tone that made me smile.

I bit my lip in an effort to keep my smile from cracking my whole face in half.

"It's simple," he said. "We have to kiss. Everyone's already talking about it, so it's a must-do situation. We might as well go ahead and take care of it."

I giggled, shaking my head, and burying my face in the blanket. "You're funny," I said.

"No," he said, casually shaking his head, "no, I'm not going for funny so much."

"What are you going for?" I asked, instantly wishing he'd answer by saying, "You."

"Turn around real quick, Claire," he said.

I turned with no hesitation whatsoever.

Cam took the blanket from off of his own shoulders, and in a sweeping, switching motion, he transferred the blanket to me. Suddenly, the blanket was around my shoulders instead of his. I stared curiously at him, wondering how he had just managed to do that. He began pulling me toward him using the hold he had on the blanket. I smiled when I realized what he was doing, and he grinned back at me, raising his eyebrows in an almost predatory way that had me feeling giddy. I made a face that showed my anticipation as he drew me closer, and he leaned in to let his face come near mine.

"If you don't want me to kiss you, Claire, now's the time to say something," he whispered.

His mouth was so close to mine that I felt little puffs of air hit my lips. I stared at him, feeling utterly desperate for him to kiss me. I had never wanted anything more. I would give up the next five birthdays and Christmases for it. Maybe ten.

"Claire, you're not saying anything," he said, after giving me several seconds to stop him.

"I know," I said after another thoughtful pause.

"You know that if you continue to stand here and not say anything, I'm gonna kiss you, right?"

Chapter 11

The blanket was wrapped around my shoulders, and Cam tugged on it, causing me to lean forward. I only moved an inch or two, but he was so close to me that even that amount was enough for our lips to touch.

He was slow and deliberate with the way he kissed me. His mouth touched mine gently, and he let it linger there for several seconds before pulling back ever so slightly. He licked his lips and smiled.

"Candy," he said.

I smiled and licked my own lips, trying to see what he was talking about. Wynn's mom had gotten a bunch of saltwater taffy at the festival, and I had eaten about ten pieces of it when we were downstairs. I had brushed my teeth since then, so I thought it was funny that he said he tasted candy. I was contemplating whether or not I brushed my teeth properly when he laughed and squeezed me.

"Earth to Claire," he said.

I flinched, pulling back just a little so I could focus on his face. Yet again, I felt surprised and confused by the way he smiled down at me like I was an object of his affection.

"I already brushed my teeth," I said, since it was what I'd been thinking about.

Cam smiled, looking like he was entertained by what a space case I was. "You must have had something on your lip," he said, licking his own lips again, which was glorious and caused the lower part of my stomach to clinch.

"I haven't tasted any toothpaste," Cam said. He paused and turned to the side so he could clear his throat. "I'll go ahead and try again just to make sure," he added with a little shrug as if he was just doing his duty.

"Try what?" I asked, but before I could even really get out the words, he leaned in and placed his lips on mine again. I wanted to kiss him so badly that I stretched upward to meet him. His mouth moved a little, and I knew he was grinning at the way I pressed against him. He let his lips linger on mine for a second or two before gently pulling my lower lip into his mouth.

"Hmm," he said, "you taste good."

"You taste good," I whispered shyly. I bit my lip and started to glance away, but he let out a disapproving sound, which caused me to reposition my face right where it had been. He smiled just before he kissed me again.

I had never seen this side of Cam—I'd never felt what it feels like for Cam Martin to take pleasure in me, and it was alarmingly wonderful. I had a hard time remembering to breathe. Cam let go of the blanket and put his hands on the sides of my face. I caught the corners of the blanket in my hands and wrapped it around his middle.

I was completely swept away, and I stared at him with an expression that I was sure made it obvious. Cam didn't leave me hanging. He leaned in and kissed me deeply, and I let him. I loved it. He set the pace, kissing me gently for a few heartbeats, and then deeply again. We smiled, and kissed, and stared, and laughed, and kissed again. There was a little talking here and there, but mostly we just stood there and kissed—both playfully and seriously. It was beautiful. If kissing were an art, Cam Martin would be one of the greats—Picasso, Rembrandt, Vermeer.

I wasn't sure how much time had passed (maybe thirty minutes) by the time Cam pulled back, smiling at me like maybe we should stop. I smiled back at him, both of us knowing what an epic kiss we just shared. I wondered if he felt guilty or if he regretted it.

"What?" he asked, seeing my wheels turning.

"Nothin'," I said with a smile.

"Let's go in," he said, pulling me toward the door.

We ended up getting into the bed together, but it wasn't what you might be thinking. I got tucked into my spot with my head on the pillow and everything, and Cam sat next to me with his legs on top of the covers and his back propped against the headboard. He was a complete gentleman who didn't even try to touch me the whole time we were laying there. Toward the end of our time together, I wound up holding his hand, but even that sort of came about by shy, "unintentional" movements on my part.

This level of touch was insignificant considering how long Cam was in my bedroom with me, which was basically all night. He didn't leave my room until 5AM, and even then, we only did it because we knew we'd be exhausted the next day.

We talked more than we had in our whole lives. He asked me about my job, and he told me about his. He knew I was a graphic designer because I'd done some work with his company. He also knew I did some drawing and hand lettering, but he hadn't really seen much of my stuff, other than the fliers and album covers I had done for Wynn over the years. Sometime around 3AM, we pulled out my iPad and looked at photos of my collection. He was really sweet about it, saying how impressive and creative all of my drawings were. He ended up drawing a picture for me just to show how bad of an artist he was. I obviously loved it and was so happy to have it in my sketchbook.

We talked about things from our childhood, and we were amazed at how we remembered some of the same events so differently. We laughed and talked and schemed all night. It was one of those times where everything seemed to be clicking into place—like the two of us would stay together, and one day, we'd rule the world. Okay, maybe not quite that dramatic, but we were clicking—really clicking.

Cam leaned over and kissed me on the lips right before he left. It was just a quick one, but it was tender and affectionate. "I'll see you in the morning," he said.

"Okay," I said, still feeling a bit breathless after his unexpected kiss. He stood up and walked around the foot of my bed toward the door.

"I had fun," he whispered, turning around to smile at me.

I sat up in the bed so that I could watch him leave. "Me too."

"Go to sleep," he said, pointing at me.

"You shoulda let me! We have a wedding tomorrow," I whispered, pointing and narrowing my eyes like he was the one who was in trouble.

He narrowed his eyes right back at me. "Yeah, and *you* kept me in here all night."

I smiled and blew him a kiss, and he grinned back, shaking his head at me as he turned for the door.

***

It was 10AM the next morning when I woke up with a jolt. "Wake up, sleepyhead!" Wynn's sister said in a bright-eyed, bushy-tailed tone.

I squinted at her silhouette in the doorway. "Alex, for realllllll?" I groaned, turning over to put the pillow over my head.

"Come on, sweepyhead," Lane yelled.

I heard the pitter-patter of his feet across my room, and then a stream of light pierced through the darkness when he threw the curtain open.

"Ohhhhhh," I groaned. "Why are y'all doing this to me?"

Alex rubbed my leg, but not in a comforting way. It was more of a *you need to get out of this bed* type of way. "We have a wedding in a little bit," she said. "You need to eat some breakfast so we can start getting dressed."

"What time is it?" I asked, sitting up when I remembered that I'd been up really late the night before.

"Aaand we have to wake up Uncoo Cam, too," Lane said as he still fidgeted with trying to get the curtains to remain open. Alex went over to help him with them.

"I was just coming up here to wake her up," Wynn said from the doorway. She had a cup of coffee in her hands, and she lifted it, indicating that she intended to bring it over there for me.

"You cannot bring me coffee in bed on your wedding day," I said, standing up to meet her at the foot of the bed. She fake kissed my cheek as she handed it to me. It was her way of telling me good morning, and I blinked and smiled to return the sentiment.

"I told them you might have been up late," Wynn said, winking at me where her sister couldn't see.

"Well, everybody needs to get up and movin' if we're gonna make it to the church," Alex said.

This triggered Wynn to break out in song.

"Goin' to the chapel,
and we're gonna get ma-a-arried"
Goin' to the chapel,
and we're gonna get ma-a-arried.
Gee I really love you,
and we're gonna get ma-a-arried,
Goin' to the chapel of looove."

Alex and I were both suckers for oldies just like Wynn, so we were all singing along by the time she finished—we busted out the harmonies and everything.

Lane watched us the whole time. He was so impressed by the impromptu musical interlude that he started bucking around the room on a fake bronco when we were done.

"Yee-haw!" he yelled excitedly as he galloped around the room.

Wynn, Alex, and I just shared a conspiratorial smile at how cute it was that he got so pumped about it.

"We gotta wake up Uncoo Cam, too," Lane said after he finished his victory lap.

"Let's go do that right now," Alex said.

Before she could corral Lane and get out the door, Wynn said, "Hmmm, Cam slept in, too," as if that were very peculiar.

Thankfully, Alex didn't even pay attention to what Wynn was saying.

"You're getting married today," I said, when Alex and Lane walked out.

"Can you believe it?" Wynn asked. "It's crazy."

"Are you scared?"

"No. I'm happy."

I smiled at her. "I'm happy for you. I think you two are amazing."

"What about you?" she asked.

I stared at her like I didn't know what she was talking about and she gave me a narrow-eyed expression. "Are you hooking up with my cousin?" she asked.

"That's not something you need think about on your wedding day," I said. I lifted the mug she had handed me. "I need to down this coffee so we can get the curling irons on."

"Alex already has all that set up in my bathroom downstairs," she said. She put her hand on my arm and looked at me sincerely. "Are you okay, Claire?" she asked.

"Yeah," I said, shrugging it off.

"I just didn't even think you and Cam... I didn't even know you even hung out as friends, so it seems crazy to think about y'all..."

"It's weird to me, too," I said. "It didn't really happen on purpose, either."

"So something did happen!" she said with wide eyes like she'd solved some big mystery.

I laughed and put my head in my hand. "I don't know," I said. "I'm delirious. I need to drink my coffee before I answer any questions. I can't be held accountable for what comes out of my mouth right now."

She giggled and then squeezed my arm in a parting gesture. "Drink your coffee and meet us downstairs," she said. "There's some stuff for breakfast in the kitchen if you want to stop by there first."

"K," I said with a smile. "I'll be right down." I lifted the coffee. "Thanks for this," I added.

"Uh-huh," she said as she left. "But it's gonna cost you." She turned to smile and wink at me from over her shoulder.

"Cost me what?" I asked.

She flexed her fingers in a dreadful pose and spoke like some diabolical villain when she said, "Detailllls!"

We were both laughing about that when she left my room.

I ran into Alex and Lane again as I was heading downstairs, only this time, Cam was with them. "Good mornin'," Cam said with a slight grin when he saw me. His voice was still sleepy, which meant it was even deeper than usual. I wanted to swoon.

"Morning," I said, trying to sound casual.

He reached out to touch me, and I just smiled and gave him a quick touch back like a mini little awkward high-five.

Alex didn't pay much attention to us, and neither did Lane. They started down the stairs hand-in-hand, leaving Cam and me at the top of them. He held out his hand as if offering to let me go down ahead of him. I started to, but changed my mind, turning to fix my eyes on him.

Every second felt like hours, and I changed my mind about ten times as to whether or not I was going to do it, but ultimately, I decided to place a quick kiss on his cheek before heading down the stairs. I didn't give him time to react or anything. I just kissed him and turned to walk away as quickly as I could. I'm not quite sure where I thought I was going, though, because Alex and Lane where only about five or six stairs down, walking at the pace of a three-year-old.

We had two different flights of stairs to go down to get to the main living area, and Cam followed me the whole time, secretly pinching, poking, and prodding at me from behind. Alex and Lane were walking a few feet in front of us, so I didn't draw attention to what he was doing. Every time, however, I would turn and give him a dirty look, which would make him smile.

I thought he would leave me alone once we were downstairs in the midst of everyone else, but he didn't. I made myself a bowl of cereal, and stood propped against the kitchen cabinets to eat it, and Cam came to stand beside me—so close that several people standing around took a second glance at us.

Cam was affectionate with me all day—even at the wedding. He was smooth about it, reaching out to touch me when no one was looking. I felt like I was in middle school again. I wanted to use any opportunity to stand beside him so that we could accidentally brush elbows or let our hands accidently wind up in the same place at the same time for a second.

Chapter 12

Wynn and Ryan's wedding was simple, rustic, and picture perfect. The whole process, including photographs, only took a couple of hours, with the ceremony itself only lasting about thirty minutes. Ryan said a few things, Wynn said a few things, and then the pastor gave the normal wedding speech about loving each other through thick and thin and always putting God first. The whole thing was brief yet beautiful, and we had some wonderful photos to show for it.

Wynn hired a local photographer who consistently worked at the chapel and knew where and how to get the best shots. He came to the house with us after the wedding to show us the photos and let us eliminate the ones we knew we didn't want. All of us gathered around the TV in the living room as Nick, the photographer, ticked through the pictures one-by-one. He was taken aback that Wynn was open to letting everyone look at them since most brides wanted a private viewing first, but Wynn was easy going like that. We went through them as a family, choosing our favorites. If someone had an intense objection to the way they looked in one of them, Nick would either delete it or tell them he could fix it in Photoshop.

One-by-one, Nick went through the wedding photos, and one-by-one, I saw for my very own eyes how obvious Cam and I were being. In fact, we were sitting on the couch together right then as the far-to-revealing pictures came up on the screen.

I felt hot all of a sudden, and I stood up.

"Where you going?" Cam asked.

I glanced back at him, feeling thankful that the lights had been dimmed for the photo viewing. "I'm just going outside for a second," I whispered, ducking out of the way. "I'll be right back. Y'all go ahead, I'm good with all of them."

Everyone went on with what they were doing except for Cam who stood to follow me. I turned to look at him once we were far enough out of the room that no one was paying attention to us. I gave him a look like *why are you following me*, which he returned with a scowl.

"Where are you goin'?" he asked.

"Wherever," I whispered. "Anywhere. I just... we just... We're being too obvious. It's too much. You need to go back in there so they don't think you followed me."

"I *did* follow you," he said. "And I don't care what they think."

I got lost for a second looking at the side of his face, at his gorgeous jaw line. His face was capable of such distraction, that for a second, I totally forgot what I was doing.

"Don't run away, Claire," he said. He reached out and pinched at the fabric of my shirt, pulling it toward him for a second before letting it go again. I wanted to collapse into his arms, but I knew I couldn't.

"Cam, we have to take a step back," I whispered. I gestured over his shoulder to the area where everyone else was sitting in the living room. "They're gonna know something's up."

"So?" he asked. "They'll be happy about it."

I shook my head. "I'm not ready... we're not ready for that. You know we can't."

He stared at me like he really didn't even understand what I was saying. "I don't see why it's a big deal," he said.

"Because it is a big deal," I said.

He took a step toward me wearing a dangerous grin. "We're a big deal," he said.

I sighed and pushed at his shoulder, trying to hold him at arm's length. For a few seconds I stared at him, and then I shook my head, hanging it in defeat. "It's too tempting, Cam. You're too tempting. I literally can't resist you."

"Then don't," he said, pulling me toward himself.

I wanted to fall into his arms. Believe me, I did. But we couldn't. We obviously couldn't.

"We can't pull your family into whatever's happening or not happening here," I said, shaking my head. "Please," I said, feeling desperate as Wynn's dad started making his way toward us. "Hey Mr. Mitch," I said as he approached so Cam would know his uncle was walking up on us.

"Y'all all right?" Mitch asked, smiling as he walked past us into the kitchen. He started digging in the cabinet for a glass.

"Fine," Cam said.

"I was just gonna step out onto the deck for a minute," I said. "I was getting stuffy."

"It is stuffy with all of us piled up on those couches," Mitch said. "Everybody's trying to see themselves in the pictures." He poured some water into his glass and took a swig of it. "They're mostly of Wynn, though, as it should be." It was then that he stopped and glanced at us as if wondering for the first time if he had interrupted something.

"I'm headed out," I said.

Cam didn't follow me. I didn't expect him to after I pretty much asked him not to. I had already changed clothes after the wedding, and I pulled my phone out the pocket of my jeans as I stepped outside.

I had a text from Wynn saying: "You okay?" and one from Cam saying: "Come back inside."

I texted Wynn back to let her know I was fine, and then I told Cam I was coming back in a minute, but that there unfortunately could be no touching, accidental or otherwise.

He text me back the monkey with its eyes covered emoji, which I had no idea how to interpret.

Turns out, it wasn't a big deal that I stepped outside. No one seemed to really even notice. They did notice that something had been going on between Cam and me, though—and it was too late for us to stop the momentum and pretend nothing had changed. We both tried our best to leave each other alone, but our newfound connection was undeniable, so we kept slipping up by talking to each other too much or standing next to each other for too long.

It was our last night in the house together, so of course, Wynn made us play a game. Ten of us sat around one of the tables and played a game called Balderdash where you make up fake definitions for things. Cam and I sat next to each other, which was a total mistake. I knew it was obvious that we were acting differently towards each other, and I was helpless to do anything to change it. I have officially learned that when Cam Martin flirts with you it is impossible not to flirt back. I spent the entire night falling prey to his charms, and went to my room afterward feeling like I'd just been tossed about in my own sea of emotions.

Cam knocked on my door fifteen minutes after I got to my room. I let him in, but I didn't let him go past the doorway. As much as I wanted to invite him into my room for a repeat of the night before, I knew I couldn't. It was too much too fast.

"I won't keep you up," he whispered, closing the door behind him. "But I want to tell you that I don't regret anything that's happening with us."

His words caused my whole mid-section to tense up.

"I want to be with you, Claire," he said. He stepped toward me, and I did the exact thing I promised myself I wouldn't do. I threw myself into his arms and kissed him. I could not stop myself. He was literally irresistible. I was not built for *Cam Martin* level of temptation. He kissed me good, and I kissed him back, and both of us were breathing heavily by the time it was all said and done.

He pulled away with a regretful shake of his head. "I better go," he said, taking a deep breath as he stretched his shoulders back.

"Night," I said.

He reached out and squeezed my hand before turning to go. "Night."

I spent the next couple of hours doing what I did every time I thought I might actually like someone… I worked myself up until I decided it would be best if I put a stop to things and go back to our lives the way they were. I hadn't had much sleep the night before and it had been a busy day with the wedding and everything, so it might have been sheer deliriousness more than anything, but for whatever reason, I came to the conclusion that it was best to put an end to things. I knew it was something I had to do, and for reasons even I don't understand, I thought it would be a good idea to do so by making a cartoon.

I composed a drawing of Cam and me at the bottom of the paper, and taking up the whole top section, was a back-and-forth thought bubble, indicating a conversation between us.

It was my way of ending things with him before we ever even had the chance to get started. I was too scared to have an actual dialogue with him about it, so a cartoon was my best option (or at least I thought so at the time).

This is what it said:

Girl: "We can't do this."

Boy: "Why not?"

Girl: "Because, I love your family, and I can't risk losing all of you if things get weird."

Boy: "They're not gonna get weird. Everything will be fine. Come on. We like each other."

Girl: "Really, it won't be fine. Let's just be friends."

Boy: "But I know you want this. I can tell you like me."

Girl: "You're right. I do."

Boy: "So what's the matter?"

Girl: "Lots of things. I've got things I don't even want you to know. Skeletons in my closet."

Boy: "Everybody does."

Girl: "Not like mine. I want to go back to things the way they were. I just need some time."

Boy: "I'm not gonna sit around and wait for you if that's what you think."

Girl: "I don't want you to."

Boy: "You suck for doing this in a cartoon."

Girl: "I know. I'm sorry."

It was a really cute cartoon rendering of us from the shoulders up with that big fluffy blanket wrapped around us the same way it was the night before. I knew the dialogue was a bummer for such a cute looking cartoon, but that was sort of the point since I hoped the drawing would help soften the blow.

I hoped the whole *skeletons in my closet* part was vague yet sketchy enough that Cam would leave me alone and not really ask me about it. I hoped we could just leave it at that and get back to our friendship the way it was. I could not lose the Martins, and things would definitely get weird if I had a fling with Cam. There was no way I could risk it.

I was nipping it in the bud as it was, and I was already going to be annoyed by his future girlfriends. Just imagine what it would be like if I let myself get any more attached to him and then we broke up. I wouldn't be able to go to any more Martin family functions for fear of meeting my replacement. Cam had some kind of hold on me. It was frightening enough that running away seemed like a better option than staying.

Sometimes when you're tired and delirious you make great art, and I stared at the drawing of us feeling happy about the way it came out in spite of the sad dialogue. Before I could think better of it, I folded it up and tiptoed down the hallway where I slipped it under his door.

I regretted doing it the instant it was out of my grasp, and I tried to get it back, but it was impossible—it was all the way under there with no hope of retrieval.

I barely slept at all that night. It had taken me forever to do the drawing, and I was so amped up from nerves after putting it under his door that I basically stayed up all night. I tossed and turned till 11AM the next morning, and we had to leave for the airport at 1.

Everybody was in such a hurry, getting packed and making plans for lunch that I just sort of fell into the hustle and bustle of it all. Cam had apparently gotten the cartoon because he didn't make eye contact with me at all. I was on the verge of crying and felt a weird stabbing sensation in my chest at the way he avoided me. I hated it so much that I felt like taking everything back and begging him to forgive me right in front of everyone. It hurt terribly to have him act like I wasn't there, but I had to remind myself that I was the one who had asked him to.

It was rushed downstairs as we all ate lunch and got our luggage into the vehicles. I went upstairs to do a last-minute idiot check in my room, and I decided to stop by Cam's room afterward. I told myself if he happened to still be in there I could do something crazy like run into his arms and do the whole beg him to forgive me thing.

I had it all planned out in my head as I walked into his room. I thought for sure he would still be in there and that my dream would come true. I was disappointed to find that his room was empty. He had obviously cleared it out and gone downstairs because none of his personal belongings were in sight.

I crossed to the area by his bed, looking for any sign of the picture I drew. I saw small trashcan near the bedside table and I went over to peek inside just in case. The thick piece of paper I had slid under his door the night before was the only thing in there. It was folded up, and I reached down to take it out, unfolding it as I stood again.

My heart dropped when I realized that it had been torn in half, straight down the middle. The two pieces ended up separately in my hands, so I matched them up as well as I could. I looked at the drawing first and was happy with how it came out, but I only looked at it for a second before focusing on the words I wrote.

I felt indescribably mad at myself as I read them. *What was I thinking telling him to leave me alone?*

I lined up the paper and strategically tore it where the drawing ended up in my right hand and the words ended up in my left. I now had a total of four pieces of paper in my hands. I stuck the two pieces of our faces in my back pocket before tearing the words into itty-bitty pieces and tossing them back into the trashcan.

I wanted to cry, but had no time to do so without putting a total damper on my best friend's wedding trip, which I clearly was not going to do. I took a deep breath, and pasted a smile on my face before heading back downstairs.

Chapter 13

Wynn and Ryan went straight to Las Vegas from Montana, and since the rest of us were headed back to Louisiana, we said goodbye to them at the airport. I did my best to act completely normal on the car ride over there and at the airport, but the dynamic between Cam and I had changed considerably that morning, and I was on edge because of it. I just knew everybody could tell that something was going on.

We had ample opportunity at the airport, and in Denver on our layover, but Cam and I never spoke to each other. I don't even think he looked at me. I was doing my best to be upbeat the whole time, but Cam wasn't. Every time I saw him, he was wearing a serious expression, which was unlike him. I was used to that smile, and I missed it. It made me sick to know I was the one who had caused it to go away.

I sat next to Amelia on our last leg home. It was just the two of us in the row again, and she wanted the window seat. I chose to sit next to her in the middle seat instead of leaving a seat between us like I did last time. I did it mostly because I wanted to be close to her. Pushing Cam away somehow intensified my need to be next to someone—maybe I was scared or something. Either way, I sat next to Amelia instead of leaving a seat between us.

"What's goin' on with you and my cousin?" she asked about halfway through our flight. I had always thought of Amelia as Wynn's little sister, but she'd grown up a lot in the last few years. I talked to her several times over the weekend, and each time I noted that she was different from the annoying little sister I used to know. I saw parts of Wynn and Alex in her, but she had her own way about her. I quite liked her, so instead of brushing off her question about what was going on with her cousin and me, I answered it.

"I think both of us just realized for a second that we could see each other in that way, but then we thought better of it." I smiled at her, hoping my answer was both specific and vague enough to keep me out of trouble.

"You've never hooked up with him before?" she asked.

I shook my head. "I don't know what made it occur to us to flirt or whatever, but it was a mistake. It shouldn't have happened. That could get weird for everybody."

"For who?" she asked. "Who would it be weird for?"

"Y'all, me, everybody," I said.

"I don't think it's such a bad match," she said studying me as if she was still forming her opinion on the matter.

"It's a bad match," I said, letting out a humorless laugh. "Just try to compare me to Jolene."

Amelia leveled me with a stare. "Apples to oranges, Claire, obviously."

"Exactly," I said.

"Exactly what?" she asked. "They're both delicious."

"Aww," I smiled and reached out to pat her for being so sweet. "I know what you're saying, and that's sweet. I'm not trying to be like Jolene or anything. It's not like that. I've just got some issues, you know? Stuff I carry around from my childhood. Stuff that has nothing to do with Cam. I know I was at your house a lot, but I had a whole different life when I was at my mom's house. I'm not a bad person or anything, I just have trust issues—not that I thought me and Cam would end up together or anything, I'm just saying…"

Amelia put her hand on my arm and stared at me sincerely the whole time I was talking. "So, you hung out with him all weekend, and then told him about your trust issues this morning?" she asked, seeing the obvious shift in dynamic.

I nodded. "Only, I didn't tell him per say."

"What do you mean?"

"I wrote him a note. A letter. A drawing."

"What was it?"

"All of those. It was a comic like I do. You know, a drawing with word bubbles."

"You broke up with him through a comic?" she asked, staring at me like I had lost my mind.

I let out a little nervous laugh as I looked around to make sure no one had heard. "I'd hardly call it breaking up since we weren't together in the first place," I whispered. "We were never together," I said, rephrasing it just so I made sure we were clear.

"I know, but y'all were all lovey-dovey at the house."

"No we weren't," I said, a little too defensively.

She smiled. "Okaaay," she said. "Well, I guess you gotta do whatcha gotta do."

"I know," I said thoughtfully. "It'll be better than letting things get awkward later."

"I didn't think it was awkward," she said. "Nobody really said anything. I heard dad asking about it one time, but that was it."

"What'd he say?" I asked.

She shrugged. "I don't even remember. He just asked if you and Cam had something goin' on, and Wynn acted like she hadn't even noticed."

I rested my head on the seatback with a sigh, feeling frustrated that there had been any drama at all. I wanted so badly to try to be with Cam, but I needed the Martins in my life, and I forced myself into believing that I couldn't have both.

None of the Martins knew about my past. They didn't know the things I'd been exposed to. I knew it was a burden they didn't need to carry, so I felt like I was doing them a favor by carrying it on my own. It had been good for me to tell Ginger, though. The things she told me had stuck with me and changed me during the last months. But the fact was that it happened. It was a scar I had, period. I didn't want to mix that part of me with what I had going with the Martins, and a boyfriend/girlfriend relationship with one of them was crossing the line into the type of territory where scars were revealed. I just couldn't have that.

"Well, my aunt Debbie was all excited about it," Amelia said, resting her head with a sigh like I had done.

"What?" I asked, my head whipping around to look at her.

She opened her eyes and smiled at my intense expression. "My aunt Debbie," she said. "She was all hopped up on the idea of you and Cam getting together."

"You just said your dad was the only one who said anything," I whispered.

She smiled and shrugged. "It wasn't a big deal. Aunt Debbie just said she wished you had been around a few years ago to save them from that Jolene crap."

"I was around a few years ago."

"You know what I mean. She was just saying she wished you two were all into each other back then like you are now." She paused and shrugged. "Well, not anymore, I guess."

I sighed, feeling more back-and-forth emotions about this than I had ever felt about anything in my entire life. "I hope your Aunt Debbie doesn't get mad at me," I said.

"She won't, she loves you. That's what I was saying."

I smiled even though I felt pitiful on the inside.

We were about thirty minutes from our final decent into New Orleans when Cam came to our row, sitting in the empty chair next to me without permission or hesitation. I shifted and pulled back to look at him, feeling breathless and choked-up. He stared straight ahead for a moment before turning to stare at me. His eyes locked on mine for several long seconds, conveying all sorts of unspoken messages.

"Seriously?" he asked. "With the note?"

I could tell he was trying to be respectful and not say too much with Amelia sitting right behind me.

"I didn't know how else to do something like that," I said. I stared into his deep brown eyes, feeling like I could get lost in them. "I certainly couldn't be expected to say all that when I'm actually *looking* at you," I whispered, gesturing at his appearance like it was obvious how irresistible he was. "I had to write it down because when I look at you... I mean... I forget how to..." I screwed up my face at him. "I'm forgetting what I'm saying right now. I can't even put a sentence together, barely."

His expression showed that he was both confused and annoyed.

Amelia, seeing that I was tongue-tied and Cam was frustrated, then tried to do to a good deed by interjecting. She really thought she was doing the right thing when she leaned in front of me and said, "She's got stuff she doesn't want to talk about with you, Cam, so just let her do her thing."

"What do you know about it, Amelia?" he asked.

"I know she was sad about the whole thing because she likes you a lot!" Amelia whisper-yelled at her cousin, getting onto him for giving me a hard time. "I know she's got some stuff happening in her life that has nothing to do with you."

Amelia, God bless her, was only trying to help me, but goodness, I wasn't prepared for how empty, how heartbroken I would feel when Cam stood up and walked off without another word.

"Was that too much?" she asked when Cam walked off. "I just know how persuasive Cam can be, and I didn't want to see you having a hard time."

"It's good," I said even though I didn't mean it. "You did fine. You were honest. I just hate to feel like he's mad or whatever."

I glanced in front of us just in case I could still see him, which I couldn't.

"He'll be fine," she said. "But I will say it seems like he really likes you."

"Oh, great, now I really feel bad," I said, looking at the rows of seats in front of us sinking my face into my hands.

"Claire, when we talked about it earlier, you were telling me all these reasons it couldn't happen, but now it seems like you regret saying that. There's no shame in changing your mind." She gestured to the front of the plane. "Why don't you just go talk to him if you want to? Tell him I should have minded my own business just now."

I shook my head, smiling sarcastically at myself for being all over the place about it. "I'm just gonna leave it alone," I said.

"Just so you know, I support you either way," Amelia said as she began to gather her belongings for our descent.

"Thanks," I said numbly.

We all had our own rides at the New Orleans airport. I had driven myself, and my car was in the long-term parking along with most of the others. Cam had done the same thing, but he didn't have a checked bag, so he left without coming to baggage claim. Just about everyone else had to wait for their luggage, and we had a good time recapping our favorite moments of the trip and saying goodbye. Part of me was glad Cam had already gone so that the tension between us wouldn't be obvious, but most of me missed him and wished he was there.

The next few days passed in the type of blur where I felt like I was an ostrich with my head in the sand. I went to work and did all the things I was expected to do, but it was almost as if I was in a hazy, dreamlike state. Most of my energy was focused on remembering everything that had gone down with Cam, and trying to decide if I had handled it correctly. I was almost sure I hadn't. As much as I didn't want to lose the Martins, I was starting to feel like a shot at Cam would be worth the risk. I would have those types of thoughts, and then I would change my mind and tell myself I had done the right thing.

I went back-and-forth like that during the days following our trip. I went to work, but I was basically just going through the motions. Even the drawings I did in my free time reflected how much I was thinking about Cam. Almost everything I drew in those days was a snapshot of moments we had at the house or funny things about me and my personal hang-ups and misadventures in love.

We'd been home for about four days when I got a call from Wynn. I was sitting in my living room with my roommate when my phone rang. I told Lilly I was going to take the call, and stepped outside as I picked it up.

"Aren't you in France by now?" I asked, closing the door behind me. It was a balmy afternoon, but there was a huge tree in the small patch of grass in the front yard of our rental house. I went and stood under it, feeling cozy like I was in a forest in spite of the cars and people who were present in my busy neighborhood.

"Vegas still," she said. "We leave in the morning."

"Are you having fun?" I asked.

"We are. My hotel's really nice. Everyone's doing a good job. Ship shape." (She pretended it was her very own hotel because of the name.)

I laughed. "Good," I said. "I hope they know who's boss around there."

She laughed. "They seriously did give me dinner comps for every night we stayed because of my name."

"Or maybe because you're famous," I said.

She laughed, still not identifying with that word even though she had an album that was currently blowing up on the Christian music charts. "They don't know me," she said, humbly. "I was callin' to see what was up with you," she added in a slightly more serious tone than the one she'd been using up to that point. "I didn't really get to talk to you when we left the wedding."

"Oh, nothing," I said. "I had so much fun, though. I thought it was perfect."

"Claire, I just got off the phone with Cam," she said, skipping the small talk. All the blood that was in my head, dropped to my feet when she mentioned his name. I felt so lightheaded that I stooped down with my back against the trunk of the tree. "Cam?" I asked.

"Yes Cam," she said. "He's all torn up."

I let out a little laugh, but it was from nerves.

"I'm serious," she said. "He called me asking what he could do to get you to come to your senses."

"Why would he do that?" I asked.

"Because he likes you, Claire. He really does. Do you like him, or were you just trying to let him down easy or whatever?"

I laughed at the ridiculous notion of anyone *not* liking Cam Martin. Of course I liked him. "I like him, obviously, Wynn, but I've got other stuff. I gotta go slow. You don't need to be worrying about this on your honeymoon, anyway."

"Well, I think you should talk to him either way," she said.

"If he wants to talk to me, he'll get in touch," I said.

"Oh, come on, Claire. I'm telling you he wants to talk to you. Just pick up the phone."

"I know, but I'm just saying... Please stop worrying about me on your honeymoon. I'll get in touch with Cam if it'll make you feel better."

"It will," she said. "I love both of y'all."

"I love you, too," I said.

Chapter 14

I wrote Cam a short but heartfelt letter that night. It started as a text, but I quickly realized I wanted to say too much.

Writing everything down was therapeutic, and I knew I would be better off for doing it even if I never gave it to him. I told him the truth in that letter. I started with how much I enjoyed spending time with him, and then I told him that I wouldn't have ended everything that was developing with us if things were normal and I was just a normal girl. Then I told him the truth about what happened to me with my uncle.

After I wrote it, I sat back and read it two times in a row, and somehow the words hit me differently as the reader than they did as the author. As the reader, I had an innate understanding that the words pertained to me but they did not define me. Ginger was right about the broken pot, and I understood it on a whole new level. They were moments in time that happened, and now I'm me, and that's all. I would gain nothing by letting that experience hinder me from living the life I wanted from this point forward.

I had handwritten the letter, and I folded the paper and put it in the drawer of my nightstand. I thought I would probably end up giving it to Cam, but I wanted to give myself a day to sleep on it just in case I regretted it. Part of me wanted to type it into an email and send it to Cam right away, but I learned my lesson on the last one. It was hard not to send it, though, because I wanted Cam to know I hadn't just forgotten all about him. The opposite was true, but how was he to know that? I couldn't believe he had called Wynn on her honeymoon to ask about me.

I thought hard about the possibility of sending him the letter digitally that very evening. I was glad I didn't do it, because if I had, then what happened next would have been really disturbing.

It was disturbing as it was, but if the letter had been sent, I would have feared the ultimate betrayal.

What, you might ask, had me all worked up?

Well, it all started when Wynn posted a few of her wedding photos to her social media. She tagged me in some of them, so I had notifications about comments. She had a lot of fans, so there were dozens of comments on all of them that she posted. I mostly scanned over them, not really paying attention to them or reading them fully until Cam's ex chimed in.

A couple of people tagged her in one of the pictures because it showed me and Cam looking straight at each other. I stared at the picture, feeling queasy at the thought of having that connection only a few days earlier and then letting it go. I also felt queasy that Jolene had been tagged in it. I instantly scrolled down and read the comments. Several different people had reached out to her about it, and she commented back to all of them with all sorts of acronyms that meant she was royally ticked off and hated my guts.

I wasn't great at social media, so it never really occurred to me to check my inbox, but there was a little number that caught my eye in the corner of the screen, so I touched on it.

It was a direct message from Jolene, and my heart sank when I saw her name as the sender. I blinked at the screen, trying to wrap my head around the fact that Jolene was writing me a personal message. Dread washed over me like a heavy wave and I found it difficult to click the button to open the message. I finally did it, and this was what she wrote:

"Listen (cuss), I could tell from day one that you were trying to get your (cussing) claws into one of the Martin boys. You need to take your (cuss) back to the (cussing) trailer park and leave the big fish for those of us who know how to fry them. Leave him alone if you know what's good for you, you (cussing cuss). You're out of your league. Your makeup and clothes looked (cussing) hideous in those pictures."

It didn't even occur to me to find humor in the fact that she had referred to Cam as a fish she was going to fry. All I could focus on were the other, less humorous parts of her message—the parts where she said things hateful enough to make me cry.

I was definitely crying after I read that.

I read it three times in a row, stopping every time on the part where she said I should go back to the trailer park. Jolene had never been to my mom's place. She didn't grow up with us. There was no way she could have known I grew up in a trailer unless Cam told her. Either that, or someone else had said it in front of her. Either way, it was embarrassing. Part of me hoped it was just a rude but lucky guess. *Trying to get my claws into a Martin boy? Really? Was that what people thought of me?*

I opened the bedside drawer and took out the letter. I was already debating on whether or not I would show it to Cam, but now there was no question in my mind that I clearly *would not* be sharing it with him or anyone else. I started to rip up the paper, but then my eye fell on a box of matches that were in the bottom of the drawer for candles. I pulled them out and used one of them to light a candle that was on my nightstand.

Once it was lit, I held the corner of the folded paper above the flame. It burned quickly, and I had to run to my adjoining bathroom to drop what was left of the burning paper into the sink. I hadn't really considered the mess or the stench that would result from burning a piece of paper in my bedroom, and I stared at myself in the bathroom mirror, cracking up about having to run in there so I wouldn't burn my hand.

I gathered the unburned corner of the paper along with some ash from the sink and floor before throwing it all into the trash. All those words that could have hurt me if used against me were now a pile of ash at the bottom of a trashcan. Thank goodness. I said a prayer thanking God that I hadn't sent Cam that letter before I got that message.

I did not respond to the message I got from Jolene. I hated conflict so much that I almost composed a message to her trying to smooth things over and telling her I wasn't with Cam, but again I made myself wait a day and think about it. I figured if I still wanted to do it the next day then I could.

I did not contact Jolene the next day or the day after that.

I pretty much did not contact anyone.

I went to work, and then I came home and went to bed. It was a difficult week for me. I hated feeling threatened or like someone was out to get me, and that's exactly what I felt like with Jolene. I had no idea what she was capable of, and I didn't want to find out.

Honestly, though, the thing that was the hardest was not having Cam—that's what stunk the most. If I had ended up with Cam in the deal, then all this hate, all this unnecessary hate would be worth it, but as it stood, I had somebody who was out to get me, and I had nothing to show for it.

I was ticked off at the world and my place in it for a few days there. It was a valley experience, as they say. I thought a lot about Ginger and the things she told me while I was going through that. Again, I remembered the story about the cracked pot, and tried to make sense of the usefulness of my past. That was difficult to do, but I had the feeling that maybe I just needed to trust that it was for something even if I couldn't figure out what it was right then.

I started coming out of my funk about a week later. It was a process, but slowly, I began getting out of the house again, and getting back to going to the gym and all the other things I did after work.

Cam didn't reach out. It hurt me that he didn't but I knew deep down that it was my own fault.

Months passed.

Wynn's album had made a bigger impact than she ever dreamed it would, and she had a few big gigs to support her rising popularity. I took a week's vacation from work and went out on the road with her on the most recent leg of her tour. She loved that because Ryan had started back to school and couldn't go with her. We went on a three-city tour of the northeast, and had a great time.

We had only been back a couple of days, when I had a message from Wynn on my voicemail. It said to call her back, so I did, and she picked up on the first ring.

"Don't make plans for tomorrow night. My dad and them just came back from Asia. He's taking us all out to Restaurant August to celebrate. I figured you'd want to get in on that."

I sighed, since that was one of my favorite restaurants, and I hated to miss it. But honestly, it might have been too soon for me with Cam.

"He's gonna be there," she said, reading my mind, "but you're gonna have to get over it sometime."

"Who?" I asked.

"Oh please," she said. "You can't possibly think I haven't noticed you've avoided everything Cam's going to since all that went down with y'all. You haven't even seen him since the wedding."

"Yeah, I know," I said, since that was an obvious and painful fact for me.

"I don't know why there's a problem," she continued. "Mom asked me if you were going, and I already told her you were."

"Why'd you do that?" I asked, feeling nervous already.

"Because you love that place, and Mom and Dad wanted you to come. They're gonna tell us stories about their trip. Come on. It'll be fun."

I thought about it for a second. "You're not gonna let me say no, are you?"

"No," she said.

"Should I bring a date?" I asked, hoping she'd tell me if Cam would have a date. It was a roundabout way to get that information, but that's what I wanted to know.

"You're hilarious," she said. "I think my cousin would murder me if I let you bring a date."

I took a quick, calming breath, trying not to seem shaken by the mention of her cousin. "What time?" I asked.

"Seven."

"Okay, I'll be there. Tell your mama I said thanks."

"I will. See you then."

I hung up the phone, knowing how on edge my nerves would be the following evening. They were already on edge so I could only imagine how I would feel walking in there.

I knew it and expected it, but that did nothing to help me deal with the crazy anticipation I felt when the time came. I was shaking in my boots as I got ready for dinner that night. I had rap music playing to try to pump me up, but I could not quit trembling. Thank goodness for extra strength anti-perspirant because I would have been sweating for sure. I did my best to calm my nerves all the way to the restaurant, feeling frustrated with myself for agreeing to come when I clearly wasn't ready to see Cam.

It was early fall, and southeast Louisiana was having our first bit of brisk weather. I wore light colored jeans and my favorite purple sweater. I was extremely nervous so I spent a good deal of time on my hair and make up. It didn't look like I had a whole lot on, but I definitely took care when getting ready because I was so anxious about seeing Cam.

I made it to the restaurant a few minutes early even though my intention was to arrive a few minutes late. About half of the family was there, but there were still several empty chairs. I chose one that already had people on both sides of me. I didn't want Cam to come in next, have the option to sit by me, and choose not to. Seems silly I know, but in the interest of honesty, that was what went through my mind when I chose that seat.

I was so anxious about seeing him that I could hardly breathe. I sat between Ms. Kathy and Wynn and didn't even think to ask until I sat down if they had been saving that seat for Ryan. Wynn patted the seat on the other side of her and said he could sit there.

Cam was the last one to come in, and he took the only seat that was available, which was right across from me. It didn't look like he had a haircut since the last time I had seen him—maybe he hadn't shaved either. He looked different and mysterious, like his recent trip to Japan had turned him into James Bond 007 or something.

Then it hit me that he wasn't being aloof or James Bond-ish at all.

It was me. I was under his skin.

Chapter 15

Restaurant August was the type of establishment with white linens. Even the water was served in glasses with stems. It had a vintage feel to it, almost like you were back in the twenties. One would feel right at home going in there dressed as a flapper. I smiled, imagining myself walking in with my hair done in fingerwaves underneath one of those beaded headbands. It made me feel nostalgic, and I played out this whole scene in my head where I was the damsel in distress and a big, tough gangster-type (Cam) busted in to save the day. There would probably be machine gun fire, but everyone would be okay in the end. I would definitely wind up in his arms in the final scene. I would say something like, "My hero," in a voice like Olive Oil.

I smiled and shook my head, laughing at myself. I looked around, trying to remember details of the restaurant so I could use them later in a drawing. I always sat up really straight when I ate at nice restaurants and tonight was no exception. I was especially mindful of my posture on account of Cam sitting right across from me. I was basically breaking my back, but a girl's gotta do what a girl's gotta do.

We ordered appetizers and then entrees, telling stories and laughing about their travels. Steve, Mitch, Cole, and Cam were the ones had just gotten back from Japan, and they had several long stories to tell, which sort of all lumped into one. They would interrupt each other and switch turns telling parts of stories like they always did in that wonderful, jovial, Martin family way that seemed like it was right out of a scene from a movie.

Cam, who was usually the star of the show, seemed a little more laid-back. He barely looked at me at first, but once our eyes caught, it was obvious that we both still felt like we had unfinished business. During the whole dinner, I went back and forth with the whole *he loves me, he loves me not* thing, but the truth was that I had no idea what he was thinking, and it was killing me.

Of course, they told the story of Cam surprising everyone by speaking Japanese. They all made him show his stuff by saying a few things. Cam had this way of balancing confidence and humility that was beautiful to watch. He delivered a whole string of words in perfect Japanese while wearing an adorable expression like he wasn't quite sure how he knew it all.

Everyone (all the women and children, at least) clapped like crazy when Cam was done, and his mom gave him a hard time about not at least telling her what he was planning. My heart dropped when she said that, and I wondered if I was the only person he told.

The conversation moved to other topics since everyone had different things going on and a lot to update each other about. Wynn's album was up for some major awards, and Ryan's best-selling book was being tuned into a mini-series. Martin Outfitters was going international, and Jacob's furniture business now had some retail space. Their territory was expanding, so to speak, and it was neat to see how they encouraged each other about it. Come to think of it, that was probably why their territory was expanding.

Ms. Kathy turned the conversation to me at one point, asking what I had going on. Some of the people at the other end of the table were preoccupied in their own conversation, but everyone in my vicinity, including Cam, looked at me as they waited for me to answer.

"Not much has changed," I said, with a shy shrug. "I'm still workin' and livin' in the same place."

"Her art is all over town," Wynn said, proudly. "This little boutique is making greeting cards out of some it, and she's gonna have an art show in December."

I smiled at Wynn and she stuck her tongue out at me in a silly expression.

"You'll have to let us know when your art show comes out," Debbie said.

"I have an invitation for it on Facebook," Kathy said to her sister-in-law. "I'll send it to you."

Debbie smiled and nodded.

"We'll all have to go to that," Liv said hearing us from the other end of the table.

I looked at Cam, hoping he'd say something like, "Yeah, I can't wait for that," but he didn't. He just sat there and looked at me with an unreadable expression. It was a surreal feeling seeing him sitting across from me. He was dressed nicely as always and, in spite of his hair being longer, he was sharply groomed. He looked like someone who belonged in a restaurant like this.

That's about when the words *trailer park* flashed across my mind. I almost heard it audibly in a low, mumbling tone like someone was saying it in slow motion. *Trrraaiiilllerrr paarrrkkk.*

You're out of your league.

No you're not. He'd be lucky to have you.

You're out of your league.

No you're not. Broken pot.

"Where is it?" Wynn asked. The way she phrased it made me know that it wasn't the first time she had asked.

"It's called The Villa," I said, assuming she was asking about my art show. "It's a small gallery. I'm showing twenty pieces. They're mostly cartoons—a couple of lettering concepts."

Wynn raised her hand. "I saw most them, and they are so cool. Y'all are all gonna wanna buy one for y'all's offices," she said, wagging her finger around the table since everyone there had an office.

"I'll buy a few of them," Mitch said with a serious expression aimed at me. He reached down and touched his pocket. "Can I just write you a check?"

"You have to wait till after the show, Dad," Wynn said.

"He can pay ahead of time if he wants," I said, making everyone laugh. I was so nervous about the conversation being turned to me that I felt suddenly overwhelmed.

"I'll be right back," I said, looking at Wynn. "I'm just gonna go use the ladies room."

And, knowing that the server was coming to take our dessert orders, I said, "Crème brulee."

Wynn knew exactly what I meant, and gave me a nod and wink as I walked away.

Every single fiber of my body hoped Cam would follow me. If it were at all possible to hope something into existence, then Cam Martin would have stood up from his place at the table and followed me that very instant. I hoped it so fervently that I had myself convinced it would happen.

I just knew he was going to do it. I saw the whole thing in my mind. I would go to the restroom, and Cam would be waiting for me when I came out. We would have an exchange in some out-of-the-way location, and he would probably kiss me and profess his love before we went back to the table.

The scene I imagined before with 20's style clothes and gangsters and machine guns came from the cartoon side of my imagination, but this scene where I come out of the bathroom with Cam waiting for me was more than that. It was a wish. I was wishing it would happen so ardently that I was actually disappointed when I came out of the bathroom and he wasn't standing there.

I kept expecting him to be around every corner as I made my way back to the table but he wasn't there either. In fact, he wasn't even at the table. My first thought was that he had indeed come after me and I had missed him. I looked over my shoulder as I sat down.

"Cam had to go," his mom explained when I got back.

"We're gonna head back, too," Alex said as she and her family stood up. "Lane's getting antsy, and so is his sister."

Cole and Liv decided heading back home wasn't such a bad idea, so they took off as well, but not before asking Debbie and Steve to order them some dessert to go and bring it by their house. Debbie and Steve agreed easily, saying they were doing the same thing for Cam. My heart stopped at the mention of his name, and suddenly crème brulee didn't seem very appetizing. I took a few bites of it once it came, but I ended up asking the server to box the rest.

Not only did my dream of running into Cam near the ladies room not come true, but he had gone and disappeared altogether. I had a distinct squeezing sensation on my chest like I couldn't get a good breath of air as I sat there, watching them finish.

I did my best to smile and talk to everyone while we wrapped things up, and of course, I thanked them profusely for inviting me to the family dinner. It didn't escape me that I was the only one there wasn't a direct family member or spouse, and I felt honored. I told them as much and hugged them all before I left. I acted like all was well with the world until I got into my own vehicle with the door closed. At that point, I let out a long, frustrated yell, pounding my fist on the steering wheel two or three times. I had never done anything like that before, so I looked around afterward, but thankfully nobody could see me.

I turned up the stereo on the way home. I turned it up so loud that it was impossible to think about anything but the music. It was on classic radio, and they played a song from the 90's called Killing Me Softly by the Fugees. I knew every word, and I sang it out loudly before singing the next one and the one after that. It was better than just sitting there being miserable about Cam leaving, which was what I would have been doing otherwise.

Maybe it was the songs that empowered me, because by the time I got home, I had decided to take action. I had been waiting for Cam to do something, but if I really wanted him, which I did, it was time that I took matters into my own hands. I knew there was no way we could move forward unless I laid everything on the table, so I had to think of a way to put myself out there.

I imagined what I would do if I were a cool girl who did cool things—things that would show Cam who I was and how I felt about him.

I decided to make a video.

I thought it would be the only way I could incorporate everything I wanted to say. It was a long shot, and may not have been be the best choice, but I had to do something, and at least it was a start.

My roommate and her boyfriend were out in the living room, and seemed like they wanted to hang out, but I excused myself, heading for my room right when I got home. I took some pictures of cartoons I had done recently—all of the ones that starred Cam. He and I had some funny moments together in Montana, and I had done a few drawings that captured them.

I set up my phone on a little bendy tripod that I happened to get the year before for Christmas. I aimed it at myself, trying to find an angle that looked right so I could film myself speaking. I shook out my hair and made some final adjustments before reaching out to push the record button. I looked straight at the little black dot at the top of my screen that was the camera since I knew that was where Cam would see me looking at him when he watched the video.

"Hello," I said, feeling like a big dork and trying to remember that I needed to speak from the heart and pretend I was talking directly to Cam. I sighed and smiled at the camera. "So, I saw you tonight at the restaurant, and I didn't get to say goodbye, and I figured I'd do this or whatever." I paused and gestured at the camera as if not knowing quite what to say. I contemplated scrapping what I had so far and starting over, but ultimately, I just continued. "Cam, I know we like each other." I said, looking right at the camera. "I know we had something, and that I freaked out and felt like I needed to stop it before we even got started." I hesitated for a second but then continued, still looking at the camera. "I'm different than you, Cam. I grew up in a trailer. My mom still lives in that same trailer. She might always live there." I glanced away from the camera and sighed before I worked up the nerve to say, "I also have this thing that happened to me with my uncle. It's gross, and embarrassing, and I never, ever talk about it with anybody. Wynn doesn't know or anything. I was little, but I remember it. I guess I'll always carry it with me. It's weird, and it's disturbing, and it's nothing like things that happen in your family, which is exactly why I felt like I needed to step away." I looked at the camera with what I hope looked like smile. "I know that me telling you this probably changes how you feel about me, which I completely understand. I just had to tell you because I could tell when I saw you tonight that you're still feeling hurt. I wanted you to know there was more to it than I told you at first. Also, you've probably noticed some of the drawings that I've edited into this video. I was thinking about putting one of them in my art show, but I wanted to ask you first since it's pretty obvious that they're me and you." I smiled and shrugged. "Anyway, let me know if it's okay. If I don't hear from you, I'll assume you'd rather me leave them out." I smiled again, not knowing what else to say. "Okay, so I guess that's it. I think you're amazing and it was really cool how you spoke Japanese tonight. I was proud of you for that, and you looked like a million bucks." I smiled and blew a kiss to the camera, knowing it was best for me to go ahead and wrap it up.

I pressed the button to stop the recording, and then I cried. I cried at the possibility of sending it to Cam and not hearing anything back. I told myself that was likely to happen. I wasn't being negative as much as I was trying to be cautious after I got burned the last time I imagined how a whole scene would play out.

I got out a few tears, and then I shook it off and went to work on the video. It took me about an hour to edit everything and put the pictures in so Cam could look at the drawings. I also strategically added some music and effects so it didn't look so homemade.

It ended up being a 90 second video when things were said and done, and I pressed the button to text it to Cam before I could think better of it.

Chapter 16

There was a big glass of water sitting next to my bed, and I pictured myself dropping my phone right into it after I sent that text. The glass was large enough to accommodate my phone and had enough water in it to devastate the interworkings—and I smiled and rolled my eyes at myself. I didn't want to be able to see how Cam responded, if he did at all, so chunking my phone into the ocean, or into the glass of water, or any other body of water seemed like a viable option.

I opted for leaving it face down on the bed.

Even if he watched the video right away, which he probably wouldn't, it would take at least three minutes for him to finish. There was no telling how long it would take him to get back to me, and the uncertainty of it all had me feeling that fight or flight affect. I left the phone where it was and went into the living room.

Lilly and her boyfriend were sitting out there. The TV was on, but they were both staring down at their phones. They acknowledged me when I came out and seemed to want to stop what they were doing so they could engage. I was anxious about the video, so I got a little chatty, talking to them for 10 or 15 minutes straight about the restaurant. I told them about Cam learning Japanese, and they used the opportunity to asked me some questions about the

Martins. They were a popular family around here—so much so that even my roommate and her boyfriend had curious little questions about them like what brand of boats they all had and other off-the-wall things like that.

Like I said, I was nervous, so I probably chatted it up more than I would have on a normal night. I had only been out there for about fifteen minutes before I went back into my room to check my phone. I wanted to give it a little while so I didn't just sit there and stare at it, waiting for a text to come in.

I sat on my bed and grabbed my phone, feeling a bit like I was moving in slow motion as I turned it over in my hand. My heart was beating so rapidly that I could feel it like the muscle it was, flexing over and over. *Bam, bam, bam, bam,* went the beating of my heart as I read the words on my screen.

Cam (3) Missed call

Cam Voicemail

The top part of my chest was bumping and thumping with how fast my heart was racing. Two of the calls had come in when I first sent the video, but the voicemail had just come in two minutes ago. I was shaking and had a hard time pressing the appropriate buttons to listen to the message.

I pressed play, put the phone to my ear, and the first sound I heard was Cam sighing.

"Claire you really can't send me a video like that and then not pick up your phone. I don't know what you're thinking. Call me back."

Cam hung up without another word, and I took the phone from my ear so I could stare down at it. He didn't sound too happy on the message, so I was especially nervous to call him back. Obviously, I had no other choice but to do it, though. I pressed the button to call him, and instantly regretted it, feeling like I should have given myself a second to catch my breath.

I hit the button to hang up before the call could connect, and I took a long, deep breath. I was in the middle of letting it out when his name flashed across my screen. Apparently, I hadn't disconnected in time, and Cam was calling me back.

"Hello?" I said, triple-begging myself to get it together and talk like a normal person even though I had trouble getting air into my lungs.

"Claire," he said, "what are you thinking not picking up your phone?"

His deep voice came through the earpiece of my phone and straight into my chest, penetrating it. Hearing his voice hit me like a ton of bricks, causing me to flop onto the bed doing my best not to squeal or something else ridiculous like that.

"I'm sorry," I said. "I didn't know how long it would take you to call me back, so I went in there with Lilly and them."

"Claire, we gotta talk, babe. You can't just tell me all that stuff in the video and then think I'm not gonna wanna talk to you about it."

I sighed, trying my best to calm my nerves. This was an impossible task since it was my most dreaded thing to talk about and I was having to say it to someone who I specifically wanted to impress. It was a recipe for disaster, and my breathlessness about it was annoying. I sighed again. "I know we have to talk about it," I said. "That's why I brought it up."

"You brought it up and then you didn't pick up your phone."

"I'm sorry," I said. "I was almost sure you wouldn't call back."

There was a pause.

"You thought I wouldn't call?" he asked, as if he might not have heard me right.

"Uh-huh," I said.

There was another pause, and then Cam said, "Claire, is this all because of whatever happened with your uncle?"

"I mean, that's certainly part of it," I said.

"What happened? Did he do something to you?"

I felt a wave of fear and shame wash over me as I tried to decide how much to say. I gave some real consideration to just aborting the mission and pressing the button to hang up.

Seconds passed.

"He made me do stuff to him," I said, finally, my voice coming out horse and barely more than a whisper. "Although, I was young enough that it didn't feel like he was forcing me. He tried to make it seem fun or whatever. Oh my God, I honestly can't believe I'm telling you this, Cam." Tears streamed down my face, but I continued talking as if they weren't even there. He couldn't see me, anyway. "I've only ever told one other person about it, and that was fairly recently. I've forgiven him and I've forgiven myself, but I know it's something that will have to be discussed with whoever I'm trying to be with, and—"

"Me," Cam said. "You're trying to be with me. And you're doing a pretty terrible job of it."

I laughed.

"I can't believe you'd even say you've forgiven *yourself* for that crap, Claire. You were a child. How old were you?"

"I don't know exactly. Probably five or six or so."

I heard Cam let out a frustrated groan when I said that. "I'd like to confront this guy," he said. "...if you'll tell me where he lives."

I let out an uncontrollable laugh since that was exactly the *last thing* I thought he would say.

"He died the other day. He was old. He wasn't my uncle. He was my mom's uncle."

"Claire, please don't ever let me hear you say you've forgiven yourself for that," he said. "I'm sorry you had to have that experience, and I'm sorry you remember it, but please do not take responsibility for it."

"Even if I don't take responsibility for it, it's still a weird thing that happened to me. It's still a strange and unsettling fact about me."

"You don't think I've seen some strange and unsettling things?" he asked. "I went to college, Claire, and I've lived in New Orleans my whole life."

"Yeah, but nothing like this," I said.

"Nothing like this exactly, but it doesn't make me feel any differently about you. I wish I could have told off your uncle before he had the chance to go and die, but it doesn't change the way I feel about you."

"You say that now because I just told you about it. You haven't had the chance to let it sink in. Just give it some time."

"Why don't you come over here right now and let me tell you something."

I covered my face with my hand as I waited to hear what he would say. "What?" I asked.

"Come over and find out."

"To your house?" I asked.

"Yep."

"Now?"

"Yep."

"What are you gonna tell me?"

"That I don't feel any differently about you because of what happened with that old man."

I paused, and then said, "You just told me."

"Yeah, but I want to say it to your face."

I sighed, thinking about how desperately I wanted to see Cam. I didn't want my past to be a part of it, either. I just wanted to see him and be normal. I told him about it, and that was enough. Maybe eventually, I'd give the details, but for now, I felt like I had said enough.

"I don't guess we need to talk anymore about what happened unless you just feel like you had some questions about it."

"That's all you," he said.

"I'm okay with forgetting about it if you are."

"I'm fine with it," he said.

"You're fine with forgetting about it, or you're fine with the fact that it happened?"

"Both," he said.

"I thought you would take a few days to think about it," I said. "Maybe it's better if you do."

"Claire, don't be ridiculous. It's bad enough that you've been avoiding me these last few months."

"It's bad enough?" I asked, with a little smile in my voice.

"Yes, it's bad enough," he agreed, smiling too. "You're coming over here," he added.

"When?" I asked, even though I knew what he meant.

"Right now."

"Oh, so that's just how it is?" I asked.

"Not necessarily, but that's how I want it to be. Bruno is still mad at me from going to Japan, and I already had him locked up for a while tonight while I went to town for dinner."

Bruno was Cam's bulldog, and I smiled when I pictured him. I considered driving out to Cam's. It was Friday night, and it wasn't late at all. *Who was I kidding? It didn't matter how late it was; I would have woken up from a dead sleep and drove over there at 3 o'clock in the morning if Cam asked me to.*

"You couldn't leave Bruno again, huh? I guess I could think about stopping by if you wanted to hang out for a little—"

"I do, Claire. I want to hang out. Why don't you get in your car and come over."

"Hey, Cam did you see those drawings I showed you on the video?" I asked, "Did you think about how you might feel about me using one of them in my—"

"Yes, I saw them... it's fine... I'm fine... You can use whatever you... We can talk about that when you get here," he said.

"Cam?"

"Yes?"

"Can you delete the video?"

"Yes," he said, without hesitation.

"It's not that I don't—"

"You don't have to explain."

"Cam?"

"Yes?"

About 10 different things almost came out of my mouth, including something about Jolene, which was just another way to give him a way out before I went over there. I decided not to say any of it.

"Yes?" he asked again while I was hesitating.

"I forgot," I said.

"Okay, get in your car and drive over here."

"It's gonna be close to an hour by the time I grab my stuff and talk to my roommate for a second."

"Be careful," he said. "Do you have gas?"

"I think so," I said, smiling at how it felt to have him checking up on me. "If not, I'll stop and get some."

"I can come by your house if you don't feel like it," Cam said, feeling bad about asking me to drive out there.

"Don't do that," I said. "I'm looking forward to seeing Bruno. I'm already trying to find my keys."

"Be careful," he said again.

"I will," I said, grinning from ear to ear.

I came really close to saying something crazy like I love you, but I didn't, and neither did he. We hung up with the promise to see each other within the hour.

Chapter 17

I changed into a sweatshirt before I went to Cam's. I loved the sweater I had on for dinner, but it seemed a little fancy for hanging at Cam's house, which was situated right on the bayou. I had filmed the video in my room while wearing a T-shirt, so I just slipped a hoodie over it when I was on my way out the door.

It was one I had found at my mom's trailer when she was cleaning out a while back, and it had recently turned into one of my favorite shirts ever. I dreaded the day when it finally fell apart. It was my brother's from his high school days. He was older than me, so it sort of had a vintage feel and look to it compared to the ones we had when I was at school there. It was one he had from football, so it said *Ram Football* across the front with the iconic picture of a ram head from the side with big, curling horns. It was a gray sweatshirt with our school logo in orange and blue as always. Micah wasn't a big guy (at least not back in high school), so the sweatshirt fit me as if it were mine. I knew I'd be comfortable in it, so I slipped it on. I pulled my hair into a bun on the top of my head since it was one of my go-to hairdos and it worked with the hoodie.

I arrived at Cam's place within an hour. There was no way to see his house from the road, but I knew exactly which driveway was his. His dad had given them each a piece of waterfront property on the stretch of land that rested in one of Louisiana's many intercostal waterways. It was only about a six-minute drive from my mom's trailer, but at the same time, it was a world away.

His long driveway wound through a stretch of woods before it led me to the clearing where he built his house. He kept a lot of the trees, even in the area near his house, so there was a real sense of being in the forest when you were out there. All of the Martins had a similar piece of property, and I had been to all of them. Cam's had always been my favorite. He built a perfect little place in the woods with lots of windows and a gorgeous view of the bayou.

Cam had been dating Jolene since he first moved in, so it was only my second or third time to go out there. I parked next to his truck and made my way from the driveway toward the house. There was a huge tree between me and the front door, and I stared at it as I walked, thinking Cam should hang a swing from one of those gigantic, low hanging branches.

"Where'd you get that shirt?" he asked from the direction of the house. I hadn't even seen that he was standing outside, so my walking came to an abrupt stop as I glanced around to locate him. He had just come off of the steps that led to the front porch and was now walking toward me on the sidewalk.

He was wearing a nice looking athletic outfit that consisted of some dark pants and a long sleeve T-shirt. Because of the industry his family was in, Cam and his brother had always set the trend in athletic apparel. His whole demeanor was one of confidence and athleticism. I was staring at how magnificent he looked striding toward me on the sidewalk when he pointed and smiled at me.

"Where'd you get that shirt?" he asked. He came to stand a few feet in front of me as we met on the walkway under that big oak tree.

I smiled at him, but he stared at my shirt like he was trying to figure something out.

"This?" I asked, staring down at it.

"Whose is that?" Cam asked, staring at it with an almost annoyed expression.

Then, it hit me that Cam played football and probably had a similar sweatshirt. I smiled as I watched him stare at my shirt, trying to figure out where I got it. He was jealous, and it made me feel giddy.

"Oh, this old thing?" I said, egging him on. I shrugged casually. "I used to date the quarterback," I said.

"Hmm, that's funny, because I was the quarterback."

I looked at him with a shocked expression and gasped. "Really?" I asked, even though I knew perfectly well that Cam Martin was our beloved all-state quarterback, the pride of Jefferson Parish, Louisiana. "You were the quarterback?"

"Yep."

I gave him a genuinely confused expression. "Then, it must have been the kicker," I said.

"Johnny Mouton?" Cam asked.

I finally broke character and laughed at that. "It's my brother's," I said. "He graduated in the eighties or nineties."

"I was gonna say... I've never seen one like that."

"You like it?" I asked shifting my shoulders around.

"I like it fine, now that I know it's your brother's," he said.

I smiled and lifted my eyebrows at him with a silly, challenging grin. "Jealous?" I asked.

He made a smirk at me. "I was about to go pop Johnny Mouton in the teeth."

I laughed at the thought of Cam popping poor old Johnny Mouton in the mouth for no good reason.

Cam and I stood there and stared at each other for a few seconds. We hadn't touched at all, but the air was thick between us. It was like we each had this area in front of us where our essence, or our energy, or whatever you want to call it, was mingling. Our bodies hadn't touched at all, but there was definitely something between us. The air that was between us was just different than the air that was in the rest of the world.

"I will zap you if I touch you right now," I said, after I had that whole chain of thoughts.

He smiled. "You mean like static?"

"Not really," I said. I stuck my finger out in an E.T. pose. "I just feel like me and you might buzz if we touch," I said, referring to the chemistry between us, which was palpable. "I think if you put us in a pot and stirred us up, lightning might come out."

"Would we just be stuck being lightning after that?" he asked.

I shrugged. "I didn't think that far."

"How far'd you think?" he asked.

"About right here," I said, gesturing around me to my current surroundings in Cam's front yard. I did a double take at the beautiful waterway to my right, knowing how crazy it was for me to be standing there doing what I was doing. *Was this really happening?*

"You wanna go check it out?" he asked, seeing me glance at the water. I nodded, and we took off. There was a path leading from his house to the shore, and we walked on it for a ways before it led us to the wooden deck that eventually became the dock. The dock was small and old, and I knew Cam had plans to build a new one eventually.

"How long has this been here?" I asked when it hit me that Cam's house was only a few years old and his dock seemed much older than that.

"This part of the land used to be a camp," he said. "It was in bad shape. We had to tear it down before I built the house. I kept the dock."

"I like it," I said, sitting down on the edge of it, near the end.

Cam sat next to me, with his legs facing the other way so that we were side-by-side, but facing opposite directions. We still hadn't touched. Both of us were being very cautious. I kicked my leg in the direction of the canoe that was tied up to the dock.

"Can we go out in that?" I asked.

"Yep."

"Right now?" I asked.

"Do you want to?"

I shrugged and nodded. "I never get to go out on the water unless I'm with y'all, and you know, with Wynn going to Austin and now living in New Orleans..." I hesitated. "I haven't been on the water in I don't know how long.

"Come on," he said, standing up to begin untying the canoe. He offered to take me out on a bigger boat, which was tied up in it's nice, covered home at his parents' house, but I refused, saying I preferred the idea of rowing out for a minute and rowing back.

It took us about ten minutes to get it untied, get in, and paddle out onto the water. I couldn't see the moon, but it was clear, and there were tons of stars. I heard the sounds of the swamp—frogs and crickets or cicadas or some other type of chirping bug.

Once we reached a nice clearing, we put down our paddles. Cam was sitting behind me, and I'd been turning to glance at him when we spoke, but once we finally stopped rowing, I spun around on my seat so that I could face him. He leaned forward, resting his hands on the sides of the canoe and looking at me with a mischievous grin.

"Hi," I said, smiling.

"Hi," he said.

"I like it out here."

"Me too."

"I think it might be good for you to be on the water," I said. "It feels like it's therapeutic or something."

"It *is* good for you," he said. "I'm sure there's something scientific to it, but I figure we can just go on the fact that it feels good."

I took in a deep breath and then let it out again. It really did the body good to get out in nature and sniff the air every now and then—at least it did me. That made me think of Bruno.

"Where's your dog?" I asked.

He gestured with a flick of his head toward the house. "Inside."

"Poor boy," I said since I'd totally forgotten about him.

Cam smiled. "He's fine. He'd be spazzing out in the boat if we had him out here."

"Does he ride in the boat?" I asked.

Cam let out a laugh. "He hates it, but he hates being left behind even more. One time, he jumped in from the dock and hit his big ole belly right on the side. Cam patted the edge of the canoe, and I shuttered at the thought. Cam shook his head and smiled. "He was fine, but he made this honking noise when he did it that was the most hilarious thing ever. He had never made that noise before, and he hasn't made it since. I tried to squeeze his sides just right to make him do it again, but it was a one time thing."

I put my hands around my middle, and gave a squeeze, trying to replicate the honking noise Bruno made. Cam laughed at me before wiggling the boat just a little to scare me. I held onto the sides and widened my eyes at him like he was in big trouble.

"Don't you dare make me come over there," I said, pointing at him as I narrowed my eyes.

He smiled. "If shakin' this boat's what's gonna make you come over here, then you better hold on," he said defiantly.

I held his gaze as if daring him to do it. "You better not," I said.

He raised his eyebrows and smiled as he gave the boat another little shake.

I raised my fists at him with that a mock angry expression, and his smile broadened.

"How'd you get way over there?" I asked feeling desperate enough to touch him that I'd say something like that.

"Scoot over," he said, nudging his chin at me. He stood to shift onto my seat in the middle of the canoe. He knew how to handle himself on the boat and made the transition look easy even though it was probably tricky. He settled next to me.

"Hi," I said.

"We're past that," he said.

"We are?"

He nodded. "Way past."

"Where are we?" I asked, hoping my voice didn't betray my breathlessness.

"We're at least at *how was your day*," he said.

"How was your day, Cam?"

"It was fine, I caught up on some things I had to do around here. Then I went to town to eat with my Dad and them."

"Oh yeah?" I asked as if I hadn't been there.

"Uh-huh," he said.

"My family forced me to sit right across from this girl."

"Oh, they did?" I asked, feeling all gooey inside.

"Uh-huh," he agreed. "They wanted me to notice her or whatever, but they didn't know she already dropped me."

"I don't think she *dropped you*," I said. "Since she never really had you in the first place."

Cam had been staring at the water, but he looked straight at me when I said that. "She had me," he said. He nudged his chin at me. "You know you did," he said, speaking in first person just to clarify.

My insides felt warm and melty. I slunk down and leaned into him, letting him catch me in his arms, which he did without hesitation. We were in a bit of an awkward position on the seat of the canoe, but we adjusted easily, and soon, I was in his arms with my face resting on the middle of his chest.

I clung to him, and he held me tightly. The way we embraced each other left no room for doubt—we were equally relieved to finally be in each other's arms. It was like nothing I'd ever felt before. It was magical. There was actual electrical wattage coming through our bodies like we'd been plugged into a socket.

Chapter 18

It was a gorgeous evening, and I could think of no other position that was more comfortable than the one in which I currently found myself. Cam and I just sat on the water, listening to sounds and holding onto each other.

We talked about my art show and which of the drawings were his favorites. He said there were a few of them that I couldn't share with anyone else at all, and I loved knowing which ones he considered intimate or special and why.

Cam had a flashlight, and before we paddled back, he shone it all around, looking for frogs and alligators by the reflection of their eyes. He pointed out several animals, and each time he did, I thought about coming across a gator, and I snuggled into him. It was the whole damsel in distress thing, only not quite to an Olive Oil level. I quite liked how alligator-phobia made him hold me closer, and I smiled the whole time, almost wishing we saw more wildlife than we did.

The middle of a boat wasn't the most comfortable place in the world, but the view and the company made it one of the most special, memorable times of my life. I had no idea how long we'd been out there before Cam said, "You wanna head back?"

"You mean to your house?" I asked, looking at the dock.

"The house, the dock... I definitely didn't mean back to New Orleans, if that's what you're thinking."

Cam grabbed the sides of the boat and balanced his way nimbly to his place at the back so he could steer us home. We had drifted a little ways, so it took a few minutes to paddle back to the dock. He tied up the boat and hopped out before offering his hand to help me. I gave him my hand as I stood, and he lifted me out of the boat and onto the dock.

"Whoa," I said, not expecting to get lifted up so quickly.

"Whoa to you," he said, settling me next to him on the dock. He smiled at me and I smiled back.

"Hi," I said since I was otherwise speechless.

He smiled and shook his head at me. "Nu-uh," he said. "No hi's. We're way, way past that."

"No hi's?" I asked, pretending to be disappointed.

His expression was one of distaste as he shook his head. "No," he said with quiet insistence. "We're so far past hi, it's not even funny."

"How far?" I asked, biting at the inside of my lip to keep from smiling.

"So far," he said, after a thoughtful pause where he mostly stared at my mouth. I wanted to smile at how long it took him to respond, but I did my best not to.

"Show me how far," I said, knowing I was daring him, and also knowing he would accept my dare.

Both of us were dying to kiss. I had been there for at least an hour, and I had no idea how it had taken us so long—it's like we were holding out intentionally to torture ourselves.

"I thought you'd never ask," he said taking a step toward me. He brought his face to the place where it was only a foot or so from mine. I tried not to give in and touch him first, but it was impossible to refrain from reaching out and making contact with him. I let my fingertips touch his cheek, starting by his ear and moving down his jaw.

"You look like this," I said, absentmindedly astounded by it.

He smiled, which made me let out an unintentional giggle at the way he amazingly enough just got even cuter.

"Yep, I do look like this," he said, pulling back an inch or two to study me. "You're beautiful," he said.

I closed my eyes bashfully and shook my head. "I wasn't saying that to try to get you to say something about my—"

"I'm not saying you're beautiful because I thought you were fishing for a compliment, Claire. I mean it. I seriously love your face. You appeal to me in a way Jolene never did." My heart was racing at the mention of her name, but Cam just stood there and studied me as if he was at a loss for words. "I don't know how I didn't scoop you up all those years ago. You're adorable, Claire, inside and out. Your nose is cute, and your eyes are amazing. They're green even though you say they're brown. Your face changes when you smile, and it makes my chest feel weird."

I glanced out at the water since it was hard for me to know how to respond to such kind words. "You're sweet to me, Cam," I said, shaking my head a little.

"It's the truth, Claire. I never knew it would happen when we were kids, and to tell you the truth, I'm not even sure how it did. I think maybe it was that day when I saw you on the sidewalk."

"I liked that day," I said.

"What else do you like?" he asked, clearly wanting me to respond by saying I liked him.

"You," I said.

"Who?" he asked, leaning in as he wrapped his hand around my back to pull me closer.

"You." I took a shaky breath as he rubbed his cheek near mine, teasing both of us by letting our mouths barely brush.

He smiled at my unsteady breath, and the way his face moved when he smiled made my knees weak. I seriously couldn't hold my own bodyweight and was thankful Cam had a secure grip around my waist. I leaned into his arms.

"You're melting," he said, grinning.

"I know, I get all woozy when you put your face next to mine like that."

"Like this right here?" he asked, rubbing his cheek on mine with a feather-light touch.

"Yes," I whispered, barely breathing.

I turned to the side, so that our mouths would come into contact. I acted like it was unintentional, so when our lips touched, they were in the relaxed position like we weren't anticipating a kiss.

"Hmm," he said thoughtfully as he pulled back to stare at me. "You tried to kiss me just now," he continued with a completely straight face.

I nodded, unashamed.

"You wanna kiss me?" he asked like was the first time the thought crossed his mind.

I nodded, still wearing a serious expression.

"You love me?" He asked, as if the answer was my ticket to a kiss.

I felt shy about answering that, so I stared at him for a few seconds, but ultimately, I nodded. It was barely there, but it was a nod.

"What?" he asked.

I nodded a little more as I glanced at his shoulder and the water behind him, and anywhere but at his face.

"You have to say it," he said.

"Then so do you," I said.

"Oh, I have no problem saying it," he said. "That's easy. I love you Claire. I know it. I feel it. It's different than anything I've ever had. You're different, and I love you."

"Cam, I'm overwhelmed by that right now," I said, being honest. "I don't mean to seem doubtful, but it doesn't seem real. Only certain types of girls usually end up with guys like you."

"Your type, I hope," he said. "Look at me, Claire," he added.

My eyes met his.

"I will never hurt you."

I pulled back an inch or two to focus on his face.

"I will only protect you," he said.

The corners of his mouth turned upward in a slow grin that made me take a sharp intake of breath on accident. He literally took my breath away.

"I want to treat you, and please you, and show you how to trust me."

I didn't mean for it to happen, but a tear gathered in my eye and rolled down my cheek at the level of sincerity he was showing me. He quickly ducked to put his mouth on the tear as it slid down my cheek, catching it in his mouth. The feel of him tasting my tears made me crazy with desire. To top it off, he let his mouth linger there. I wrapped my hand around the back of his head, holding him close to me.

"I'm not claiming to know what love is, because I think I'm kind of a novice at it," I said, being honest. "But I do think I love you, Cam. I'm excited to try to at least."

He smiled as if that was good enough, and I smiled back at him. We exchanged a lot of promises in that eye contact. I knew he loved me, and he knew I loved him, too, in spite of my ineptitude with saying it.

"Kiss me already," I said, in a purposefully breathless tone

His smile faded just before he let his mouth touch mine. Our mouths were not loose this time. This was no accidental contact. This kiss was very intentional. Cam's mouth was slightly open when it came down on mine, and he bit at my lip, pulling it into his mouth right away. He repeated the process three or four more times, kissing me a little longer each time.

"Aww, Caaaam," I squeaked out, feeling dizzy with desire after that last kiss. He must have liked the sound of me saying his name, or maybe he could just hear how desperate I was by my tone... either way, he pulled me closer and kissed me like I'd been imagining.

I had the thought the last time he kissed me that he was the worlds best kisser, but somehow it still surprised me that he was so good at it. He took complete control, kissing me gently and tugging at my lips before smiling at me and kissing me deeply again. It was a perfect experience, standing out there on that old, rickety dock, feeling like the apple of Cam Martin's eye.

"Did I tell you I love your face?" he asked, pulling back after we kissed.

I nodded shyly, and he leaned in to kiss my nose.

"I like your nose, and your cheeks and your chin." He leaned in to kiss all of those places, and I stuck them out one-by-one, letting him. He smiled, which made me smile. "And your smile," he said, letting our lips touch even though we were mostly still smiling. One, two, three, four more kisses like we were trying to stop but just couldn't.

"We better go get Bruno," he said, finally.

"Oh, poor Bruno! I forgot all about him."

"You're gonna have to be a better mom than that," Cam said, causing a comfy feeling to come over me like a blanket. It didn't matter that it was in reference to a dog, hearing the word mom being used to describe me felt right—especially when Cam said it. For the first time in my life, I not only felt like I could see myself as a mom, but that I might actually be good at it. In fact, I was looking forward to it.

All these feelings of family and future caused me to instantly fear that what I had with Cam was capable of disappearing as quickly as it came. I was tempted to be insecure about Jolene, or my past, or any number of things I could have chosen to be insecure about, but I made a conscious decision to push those things out of my mind. I was me, and that would have to be enough.

I smiled at Cam. "I'm gonna tell Bruno I'm sorry for forgetting about him," I said, as he pulled me toward the house.

"He'll forgive you if you give him some peanut butter."

"I'll definitely give him some," I said.

"Do you have any?" Cam nodded.

We were holding hands as we made our way up the path toward the house, and he tugged on my arm to swing me forward, twirling me around. I went with it, dancing with him as we walked.

The huge, sprawling branches of his oak tree caught my eyes as I turned around, and the first thing I said when he caught me up in his arms was, "I'm gonna hang a swing in this tree, you know."

"Oh yeah?" he asked.

I nodded. "It's a shame that there's not one already. We'd go on there right now."

"You mean a piece of wood with some rope?" he asked, staring at the tree as if he could just whip that up at 11 o'clock at night.

"A porch swing," I said. "I always wanted to hang a porch swing from a tree like the one in the Broussard's yard." I looked at the branches and was able to imagine exactly which one I'd choose to hang a swing. I pointed at it. "That one," I said. "You could hang a nice, big swing on that one."

Chapter 19

I stayed at Cam's house until 1AM. Cam had to get up early for a game of golf in New Orleans with one of the company's distributers. His brother, dad, and uncle were all going, and they had to get on the road early.

I had so much fun being with Cam that night. I couldn't get over how different it was than when we were growing up. He was still the same up-beat, outgoing person he always was, but his attention and affection was focused on me, which changed the types of expressions he made when he looked at me. I was done for.

I went to my mom's when I left Cam's house. I almost decided to make the trip back to New Orleans, but my mom's place was close, and it would give me an excuse to have coffee with her before I left in the morning.

My old room was full of stuff, including a treadmill and some other work out equipment that I almost tripped over when I came in, but otherwise it was the same as it was when I was in high school—posters and all. I stared at one I had taped to the ceiling for what felt like forever.

It took me so long to fall asleep, that several times, I got frustrated with myself for not just driving back to New Orleans. It was after 3 when I drifted off, and I didn't wake up until 10 the next morning with my mom gently squeezing my leg. Her hair was pulled into a ponytail and she had on her work shirt, a blue polo with the bait shop logo on the lapel.

"I was tryin to letcha sleep, but I gotta be at work in thirty minutes, and I wanted to tell ya good mornin'."

"Mornin'," I moaned sleepily, blinking at the Hello Kitty digital clock on my bedside table. "It's Saturday," I added, stretching.

"I'm workin' today and tomorrow. It's one of our busiest weekends with that fishin' tournament."

I sat up, gathering my wits and remembering where I was and what was going on. Flashbacks of the night before with Cam began playing in my mind, and an uncontrollable smile spread across my face. My mom gave me a curious glance, but she didn't ask why I was smiling.

"Why'd you come in so late?" she asked.

"I was down the street with some friends, and I didn't feel like driving back into town so late."

"Wynn?" she asked. "Erma Jean and them ask me about her all the time. They're real big fans of her music. They know y'all are friends, and they just think it's so cool that she's doing so well."

"It is cool," I said.

"Is that who you were out here visiting?" My mom asked as she straightened up some of her own clothes that were lying on the end of my old bed. "I thought she was living in the city."

"She is," I said. "I was over at Cam's."

My mom knew exactly who I was talking about when I said Cam. The Martin boys were basically local celebrities, and her eyebrows went up the instant I said his name. That made me smile.

"Do y'all have something going on?" she asked.

"You can't mention it to anybody," I said, avoiding the actual question.

"Are you dating Cam Martin?" she asked with wide eyes like she was really impressed.

I narrowed my eyes playfully at her. "Would you be so surprised if I was?" I asked.

"No," she said. "He'd be lucky to have you. Are y'all?"

"I think so," I said.

My mom was more excited about Cam than anything she'd been excited about in a long time. I honestly didn't think it would be the type of thing she'd be interested in, but she was genuinely stoked about it. The funny thing was, I could tell she was happy for me, not just because of the status of who Cam was, but because she thought he'd be good to me. She wanted me to have a better life than she did. I could tell that was her motive when she asked me about him, and it made me feel happy that she was looking out for me.

She left a few minutes later, and I picked up my phone to check it before I headed home. I looked at the photos I had taken at Cam's the night before—a few of Cam and me, some of Bruno and me, and some of just Bruno. I loved Cameron Martin and his dog so much that I almost cried from joy as I stood there looking at the photos.

I sent a text to Wynn that said: "OMGosh, I think I'm in love!"

I attached a photo of me and Bruno, knowing Wynn would put all the pieces together.

I dropped my phone in my purse, and started across my mom's trailer to put on my shoes, and hit the road. My phone started ringing right away, and I stuck my hand in my bag to fish it out.

"Is that Bruno in that picture?" I heard Wynn ask the second I picked up the phone.

"Good morning," I said.

"Claire, is that Bruno?"

"He likes it when I call him Boo-boo," I said.

"Cam's dog?" she asked since I still hadn't given her a straight answer.

"Yes." I said.

"Are you over at Cam's?" she asked sounding confused.

"No."

"I was gonna say, because I thought he was golfing with Dad and them. That's where Ryan is, too. I came out here to Mom's."

"I'm over at my mom's," I said. "I was just about to head home."

"You're at your mom's? Why don't you come over here?"

I didn't have any reason to get back to the city right away. "All right. Is it just you and your mom?"

"Alex and the babies might come over later, and I think Liv and them, too. Come on. Mom's cooking lunch. I was gonna call and ask if you wanted to come before I even knew you were at your mom's. Did you stay at your mom's last night? When'd you see Bruno? Did you hang out with Cam?"

I laughed at her onslaught of questions. "I'll be over there in a few minutes," I said since I didn't feel like explaining all of it over the phone.

Wynn met me at the door when I walked up to her parents' house. She was wearing a huge grin that made me smile and shake my head at her. "Are you gonna be my cousin by marriage?" was the first thing she said.

"Wynn, don't," I said even though I secretly loved it.

She hugged me. "Where'd you get that shirt?" she asked, looking at my Rams sweatshirt.

"My brother's closet."

"I like it," she said. "How'd you end up spending the night out here?" she asked me as we rounded the corner into her mom's kitchen—a place where I had spent more time than in my own mother's kitchen.

I crossed the kitchen to hug Ms. Kathy. "Hey Mama K," I said.

"Hey sweetheart," she said, hugging me back. "It's good to see you two days in a row. It had been a while before that."

"Was it just last night that I saw you at the restaurant?" I said, feeling out of it.

She smiled, and Wynn poked at me as I crossed the kitchen in search of coffee. There was already a pot made, so I just grabbed a mug and helped myself to some of it since that's what I always did.

"When'd you see Bruno?" Wynn asked, dying to know what was going on.

I grinned, and I lifted the mug to my mouth in an effort to hide it.

"Claire, oh my, Claire you are..." Wynn pointed at me and looked back and forth from me to her mom. "Oh my goodness, this girl is... do you see this? Claire, you are so cute right now."

"That is just too sweet!" Kathy said.

"Y'all better stop," I said, shaking my head at them and burying my face behind my hand since I knew I was blushing.

"Claire," Wynn said, pushing at my leg. "You love my cousin, don't you?"

"You better stop, Wynn." I shook my head at her before shifting my focus to her mom, who was also looking at me and smiling.

"Does your mama know?" Kathy asked.

I shrugged. "I told her we hung out or whatever." I tried to act nonchalant, but my heart was beating a thousand miles an hour just talking about him.

"Does Debbie know?" Kathy asked.

I gave her a *please calm down, Mama K* look because we were close enough that I could do something like that.

She laughed. "Debbie's gonna be thrilled!" she said. "She's the main one who told us to leave that spot open for Cam last night at the restaurant."

We talked about Cam for the next half hour or so. I told them mostly everything about how it went down, leaving out personal details but giving them the timeline of the way we'd been bumping into each other recently. Kathy and Wynn both went on and on about how much they approved of the match, which obviously made me happy.

Alex came over a little while later with Lane and baby Rosa in tow. Wynn and I put three of those huge floor puzzles together with Lane while Kathy and Alex stayed in the kitchen, working on lunch. We had just finished the third puzzle, and I had been there for over two hours when I said, "I better get going."

Wynn looked at me like I was completely off my rocker. "Why?" she asked.

"Because y'all are gonna be eating lunch soon."

"Yeah, when the *boys* get here," she said, still looking at me funny.

"He doesn't expect me to be here," I said, shaking my head. I looked down at my hoodie. "Plus, I'm wearing the same thing I was when I saw him last night. I didn't plan on staying. I was just gonna hang out with y'all this morning, and leave before they got here."

"You know Cam would want you to stay," she said impassively.

"I know he wouldn't mind me being here, but I'd rather take a shower and not be looking all rough when I see him. I'm nervous enough as it is."

"Why is you newvous, Aunt Claiwe?" Lane asked.

He was busy with the last few pieces of a puzzle and I hadn't even realized he was listening. I looked at Wynn with a doubtful expression, trying to remember how much I had just said and wondering if he'd repeat any of it.

"Because that happens to girls sometimes," Wynn said, reaching out to tickle her nephew. He laughed and squirmed, and forgot all about what he was asking me, thank goodness.

"Why don't you finish up the puzzle, buddy?" Wynn asked, looking at Lane. He nodded and she stood up, gesturing for me to follow her. I did so without question since I was planning on getting up anyway.

Instead of going towards the kitchen like I thought we would, Wynn headed for the staircase that led to her old room. "Come on, I still have some good clothes in my closet," she said.

"Nooo," I said, shaking my head and pulling my arm out of her grasp. "I can't," I whispered since I thought we were close enough that Lane could still hear. "Cam thinks I'm at home. He said he'd call me later today. It'd be weird if I'm over here when they get back."

"Just text him and tell him you're here." She held out her hands as if indicating our surroundings. "This is something you'd be doing anyway, Claire. Even if Cam wasn't involved, you'd still be over at my mom's house eating lunch."

"I know, but I'm nervous, and I have on last night's clothes."

"Just go up there and take a shower," she said turning me manually by the shoulders. "Cam would be ticked if he knew you were even thinking about leaving right before he came over. You know I'm right about that, so just getcha 'lil butt up those stairs and take you a 'lil shower, or whatever you gotta do to smell pretty."

I smiled and shook my head, knowing she was too stubborn to let me leave, and feeling thankful that was the case. I showered before I put on the same jeans I had on the night before and raided Wynn's closet for a shirt. I layered a teal, plaid, button-down shirt over a white tank top and rolled the sleeves a couple of times. It was a shirt Wynn wore in college, and I always liked it, so I figured it was a good time to try it on. My hair was damp, so I put it in a loose braid over one shoulder and tied it with a ponytail holder I found in Wynn's drawer.

I heard raucous male voices when I opened her bedroom door, and my heart instantly began humming. There was laughing, both male and female, and my anticipation grew to scary levels yet again.

Chapter 20

Cam was not in the kitchen with everybody else when I got downstairs. I was sad and relieved at the same time. Not seeing him there made it easier to breathe, but I was obviously bummed.

Within seconds of coming downstairs, I had already put a name to every face in the room, and none of them were Cam. There was even a guy I didn't know (who I assumed was their business acquaintance), but no Cam.

"Hey there, Claire I didn't know you were gonna be here," Wynn's dad said.

"Hey Mr. Mitch," I said, waving a little.

"This is Dan Dixon," he said, gesturing to the one guy in the room I didn't know. We shook hands while Mitch said, "Claire's our daughter's friend who's more like an adopted daughter, I guess."

"I have one of those myself," Dan said in that super friendly way that let me know he was doing his best to impress the Martins. People always acted like that with them.

Liv had come over with little Jude, so he and Lane were running around making airplane or truck noises or some other vehicle with a motor.

"Let's take it outside," Jacob said, corralling the two of them onto the deck.

Everyone was getting into their own two and three person conversations when Wynn turned to me and said, "He had to go by his house and take care of Bruno."

"Who Cam?" Steve asked, hearing Wynn. "He promised Jude he'd bring his dog over here."

Cole scoffed. "Jude's tryin' to talk me into letting him get one, but every time Cam brings that big bulldozer over, it just reminds me why I don't."

"Poor Bruno," I said, taking up for him. "He's a good boy."

Steve laughed at me, shaking his head. "When he's sleeping, maybe."

"At least he's a stud," I said.

Dan Dixon brought up his dog, which was one of those Oodle mixes everyone was into nowadays. He was telling us about it when Cam opened the front door and Bruno came bounding into the house.

"Better hide your kids and your wives!" I heard Cam yell from the doorway before he could even see any of us.

"You're lucky I'm holding Rosa, Cameron!" Debbie called from the adjoining living room as the dog ran past her.

Bruno kept running, taking a lap around the whole kitchen and living room like a maniac. "Put him outside with the kids!" Cole yelled as Bruno ran past. "Jacob's out there with them."

I bent down to touch Bruno's back as he ran past me going about a hundred miles an hour, and looking like a big, round Pac-man. By the time I stood up, Cam was standing where I could see him.

I could tell he had been golfing. He had on some khaki pants with a collared shirt. He had untucked it most of the way, but I could tell by the creases on the bottom that it had been tucked in while he was playing. He stared straight at me with a perplexed expression like thought he might be seeing things, and I smiled.

Bruno continued running around greeting everyone, but Cam's attention was fully focused on me. Everyone else in the room was trying but failing to ignore us. I could tell, even from my periphery, that they were curious about us.

Cam ran a hand through his hair before tossing his keys onto a nearby table. He smiled and opened his arms before he flexed his hands at me, motioning for me to come to him. I smiled and widened my eyes, telling him I was embarrassed to cross the room in front of everyone. He just shook his head a little as if saying that was too bad. He flexed his hands again, telling me a second time to walk over there.

I was so crazy about him and wild with nerves that I almost felt a pulsing sensation as I walked toward him. I knew most of the others were watching us, and I didn't even care. I just stared at Cam with a smile as I crossed the kitchen, and he stared back at me like there was about to be some PDA when I finally got over there.

I shook my head almost imperceptibly, warning him to be good, and he shook his right back, denying my request. I smiled at him for being so impossible.

"Cam was asking if he could have that swing we have in the shed," I heard Steve say from behind my back.

"Do you want it?" Debbie asked. "It's five foot, I think."

I walked up to Cam as his mom was talking about the swing, and he looked straight at me. "You wanna go look at it?" he asked.

"It's a nice one," Debbie said. "It's Amish made. Where you planning on puttin' it?"

Cam looked at me as if I might answer, but when he saw the look of utter terror in my eyes, he smiled and said. "In that big oak by the house."

"You might have to paint it. It's always been under a patio, so I don't know how it'd do in the weather like that. I don't think we treated it."

"It'll be fine," Steve said. "That wood's already treated. You'll just need to get some chain. It'd be worth measuring. I bet you'll wind up needin' more than you think."

"I have a bunch of rope that'll work for that," Mitch said.

The whole family went on talking about how and when they would hang that swing, and I looked at Cam with a stunned expression, unable to believe that this whole conversation had just gone down.

He grinned at me before reaching out to pinch at my shirt. I stepped forward, and he pulled me into his arms.

"You didn't tell me you were gonna be here," he whispered close to my ear. "I didn't even see your car out there."

Everyone else did their best to ignore us, but it didn't really matter because I could only see Cam.

"It was an accident that I stayed," I said. "I haven't been home yet. Wynn asked me over this morning, and I ended up staying till—"

"I'm happy you're here," he said. "I think you should probably just move in with Aunt Kathy and Uncle Mitch until I marry you and you move in with me. I was dreading you being in New Orleans when I came home today."

I smiled. "How was golf?" I asked, since I was too shaken up to know how to respond to his sweetness.

"Fun. Like it always is when you win," He said that last part for the benefit of his brother who had just come to stand near us with his freshly made plate of food.

Cole smiled and shook his head. "You come talk to me in a few years when you have a toddler running around, wanting to wrestle you all the time and waking you up at six o'clock every morning."

Cam cringed and looked at Liv, who nodded in confirmation to her husband's story. "Just get him a dog," Cam said. "That'll wear him out real good."

"See, honey, it'll wear him out," Liv said, cuddling up next to Cole and placing a kiss on his cheek. Cole smiled and rolled his eyes at her, as if he knew she and Jude would probably end up getting their way.

Cam and I were making physical contact but I wanted to curl up next to him the way Liv did with Cole. I wondered when I'd feel that I had the liberty to do that with Cam. He pulled me closer as if he knew what I was thinking.

"I can't believe your dad's trying to help you hang that swing today," I said.

Cam cozied up next to my cheek and neck, breathing in like he loved how I smelled. "We like to go ahead and get stuff done while we're thinking about it," Cam said absentmindedly as he hugged me.

I giggled and squirmed a little even though I didn't want him to let me go. "I'm so excited to see it," I said, still whispering since everyone was close by. "Do you mind if I stick around while they..."

I trailed off because Cam furrowed his eyebrows. "Claire," he said. "Of course I don't mind if you stick around. I'm hanging it for you, after all."

"Don't do that," I said. "I mean, unless you want it, too."

"If that old swing in my parents' shed somehow makes a *you* magically appear on it, then you better believe I'm hanging it." He paused and looked down to focus on me with a serious expression. "Will *you* appear on it if I hang it from the tree?"

I nodded.

"Then I'm hanging it," he said. "Consider it hung."

Liv and Alex both agreed that they would like a swing hanging from a tree if they could decide on the right one. They tried to imagine and explain different possibilities to each other about trees on each of their properties. This started a conversation about native trees in which the guest, Dan Dixon, ended up having plenty of questions and comments. Steve and Mitch knew a lot about Louisiana forestry, and they explained some of the native trees and animals to Dan.

They told him the legend of the Spanish moss, which hung from many of the trees in our area. There were a few different stories about it, and they varied from family to family, but they all had to do with love, and tragedy, and someone's hair being cut and spread into the trees where it continued to grow and became the moss we see today. Steve told one version of the story where a man's beard was what got it going, and then Ryan told the one he knew about it being started by the hair of a beautiful princess. Ryan, being the historian that he was, told the story beautifully, and by the end of it, we were all convinced that the princess legend was absolutely accurate.

The whole crew, including Dan, went on the fieldtrip to get the swing and hang it in Cam's yard. The limb was only about ten or twelve feet off the ground, so Cam climbed up there, straddling the giant limb as he coordinated efforts with the guys below, and adjusted the ropes. He didn't seem intimidated at all. I, on the other hand, hated seeing him up there, and cringed the whole time.

Start to finish, the job took them a couple of hours, and at the end of it all, we were left with a gorgeous, Amish made swing that was suspended by smooth-swinging rope. Everyone left after we were done. Wynn and Ryan stayed the longest, but even they were on the road headed back for New Orleans within an hour after the swing was in its new home.

"Cam," I said from my spot on the swing.

It had been a few minutes since Wynn and Ryan drove off and Cam was standing near the front porch, whittling a piece of wood with a pocket knife. I had been closing my eyes on the swing, so I hadn't even noticed he was doing it until I called his name and opened them.

Bruno was stretched out on the porch, completely passed out, and even though I didn't want to, I said, "I can't always stay on your swing, you know. I have to get back to my house at some point."

He shook his head. "No, you said you'd be on the swing if I hung it."

I giggled, laying my head down and closing my eyes again. "Whatcha makin'?" I asked with my eyes still closed.

"Nothin'," he said. "Just sharpening a stick for fun."

I let out a laugh at that. "I might wanna try," I said. It took me a minute to stand up and cross over to him. He had changed into a T-shirt and jeans for his tree-climbing excursion, and his T-shirt had green and brown stains on it from where he had to shimmy up the branch. I smiled thinking about what a big dork I was for liking the stains on his shirt. I reached out to take the stick and knife that Cam was offering as I approached.

"Hold it away from you," he warned, even though I already knew that.

I imitated the motion he'd been doing, chipping away at the end of the stick like I was sharpening a pencil. "That's fun," I said, handing it back to him after about ten or twelve swipes at it.

He took the knife from me, smiling as he closed it and dropped it into his front pocket. He held up the slender, straight stick, and I caught it between my middle and ring fingers. Cam positioned his hand against mine with the stick going through his fingers as well. Our hands were palm to palm with the stick going right through them. It looked like an arrow piercing our hands and I tilted my head from side to side loving how it looked.

"I'm definitely gonna draw this," I said.

"It needs a little feather on the end," he said.

"I'll add a feather," I whispered, turning toward him. We were in such close proximity that even a silly phrase like *I'll add a feather* seemed intimate. I barely breathed as I took in his face, which was right next to mine. "What color?" I asked.

He shifted to stare at me. "I get to pick the color?"

"Or I can," I said.

"Surprise me," he said.

"Do you like red?"

He smiled. "I like surprises."

Epilogue
The following December

It had been a few months since Cam and I had been seeing each other, and we'd been as inseparable as we could, considering the fact that our houses were an hour apart and we both worked full time. We still saw each other almost every day, which was amazing. What's more amazing was that I missed him really bad on the days I didn't see him. I had gone from not even considering Cam Martin as a romantic possibility, to not being able to imagine my life without him.

I was surprised to find the transition from Wynn's friend to Cam's girlfriend was an easy and natural one for both the Martins and me. No one ever mentioned Jolene, but I could tell by the way they treated me that they were happy Cam and I were together. They were also extremely supportive of my creative endeavors and would all be at my art show later this evening.

I went for a red and white feather when I drew and painted the picture of our hands with the arrow. Most of my original art was pen and ink, (therefore no color) but I'd been known to add some watercolor here and there where I saw fit, and the drawing I did of our hands holding the stick was one that needed color. I also painted a heart in the background since it fit the design.

It was one Cam was okay with me showcasing at the gallery. By the time December made it around, I had so many new pieces that it was hard to narrow it down to just twenty. I talked to the gallery owner, and she said it'd be no problem for me to show thirty of them since most of my pieces were no larger than 11x14, even with the matting and frames.

So, I chose thirty pieces, and with the help of several other people, I hung them in the gallery just this morning. Tonight was the official opening, so there would be refreshments and I would probably be expected to say a few words.

Public speaking was a severe fear of mine, so I told Paula (the gallery owner) that I'd probably just walk around and talk to everyone individually, that way I didn't have to address them all at once. She agreed, but seemed a little taken aback that I didn't want to do it. I told Cam about her reaction, and he encouraged me not to be afraid. So at this point, I was 50-50 on whether or not I would go through with making some sort of speech. I would probably suck it up and do it, but I liked telling myself that I had an option not to just in case I got there and froze up.

"Why are you going this way?" I asked, when Cam turned down the wrong street on our way to the gallery.

Cam looked at me from over the console with a smile and then glanced at the clock on the dash. "You can't be early," he said. "They're expecting you to show up at eight. You have to give them a chance to get there and check out the stuff for a minute."

"Fashionably late?" I asked, nervously checking myself one last time in the mirror.

"No, just fashionably on time," he said. "I thought I'd go by that corner where we ran into each other since it's over here not far from Villa."

"I actually went by there this morning on my way back from hanging everything. You'll never believe it."

"What?" he asked.

"That lady. The one that made me hug everybody... She wasn't even there. That house is for sale."

"No it's not," he said.

I stared at him from across the console with a perplexed look on my face. "I just saw it this morning. There was a sign out front."

"I mean it was for sale, but it's not any more. Jacob bought it. I think Caleb's planning on living there. They're gonna make that whole side yard into a workshop and give demonstrations and stuff. I'm not sure what all they have planned."

"You're kidding," I said as we passed the blue house and I stared at it.

Cam shook his head. "I heard him talking about it yesterday. Their stuff's been doing well at Keller's, and they like the neighborhood, so it works out. I was gonna take you by there to tell you, but I didn't know you already went by this morning."

"I was actually going by to see that lady, you know, to bring her a Christmas card. I was shocked she was gone."

"You can still drop it off there," Cam said. "Jacob will get it."

"Or Caleb," I said. "I found her business cards in my wallet," I said. "I had two of them—one that I'd picked up on my own, which had her street address on it. And a second—the one Ginger handed me when she told me to send a Christmas card. This one had a PO box on it."

"Really?" he asked.

I nodded, and he shrugged.

"Maybe she knew she was moving," he said.

I didn't say anything, but I nodded when he glanced at me.

We pulled into the parking lot at the gallery, and I was extremely nervous. Just judging from the parking lot, there were more people than I expected.

I sighed. "I can do this," I said, somewhat doubtfully.

"You got this, easy," Cam said. He reached over and squeezed my leg before opening his door. "Nothin' to it. Just smile and take all the compliments as they roll in."

I squinted at him like he was being silly even though I loved the way he encouraged me. He jogged around to my side of the truck and was there by the time I got out. We talked on our way to the front door of the gallery, but I was so out of it that it was just small talk about how I should have worn a thicker jacket.

There were at least fifty or sixty people filling the front two rooms of the gallery where all my art was hanging. A few people, including Wynn and my mom and brother, came up to me when I first walked in, but most people hung out wherever they were standing there like they were content to mingle with each other and not have to be entertained by me. This was a relief. I think I assumed everyone would look right at me, waiting for me to say something right when I came in, but they didn't. I heard some hushed whispers about my arrival, and I smiled at myself for enjoying a little taste of the glory.

It took Cam and me a few minutes to take off our coats and speak to everyone who was standing by the door. He stayed right next to me as we began making the rounds. All of the Martins were there, including Nana and Pops. Amelia had finished her finals early and just flown home for the holidays, so she was there too, along with one of her "friends" from school, who happened to be a young, handsome guy that was also a marine biology major. I met him and talked to Amelia and several other people before Cam and I made our way into the second room.

I glanced around, taking in the groups of people standing around, and trying to decide which direction to go first. Cam pulled me to the right where we stood, talking to a few people they had invited from Martin Outfitters.

I noticed that some of the people in the first room started making their way into the second room. It wasn't a big deal at first, but after a minute or two, I started to feel like they were gathering on purpose, which made my heart start racing even faster than it already was. No one was looking at me or anything, but it was growing increasingly crowded in there. I started to get the heebie-jeebies, feeling like I wanted to go back into room one.

"They're all in here," I whispered where only Cam could hear.

"They love your art," he whispered back. "They just want to look at it."

I glanced at the piece that was closest to us. It was one I had done...

Wait a second.

I stood there, staring at the piece in front of me, wondering when exactly I had done it. I felt like I was going crazy, because I honestly didn't remember drawing it.

All the blood left my face as I stared at it. I was relatively sure most of the conversations in the room had ceased and people were now staring at me, but I didn't care. It was exactly my style, but I had not done this piece of art. In fact, I'd never even seen it.

The subject matter was obvious.

There was no other way I could take it.

There, on the wall in front of me, was a cartoon drawing of Cam and me in an art gallery—this art gallery.

He was down on one knee, holding a small box with a shiny, overly-large, cartoon, diamond ring, and I was making a shocked but overjoyed expression as I stared down at him with my hands clasped in front of my chest. There were hearts coming out of my head and a word bubble that said the word 'yes' with an exclamation mark.

I stared at it for what must have been at least ten full seconds before I realized that the room had gone completely silent. Tears began stinging my eyes when I realized what was going on, and by the time I turned around, there were already streams of them falling onto my cheeks.

I knew what I would find when I turned around—the exact scene from the picture—only my hands were clutched in front of my face so I could try to hide the tears.

"Who drew this?" I asked, looking out at the crowd of people standing all around me, and pointing to the drawing.

Cam cleared his throat when I asked it, which made everyone else in the room laugh.

I looked at him. He was my knight in shining armor, down on one knee with a ring box just like in the cartoon. And just like that, everyone else in the room disappeared. When I looked at Cam, I no longer cared about everyone else. I no longer cared who drew that picture or who hung it on the wall. I realized as I looked at Cam that all my questions could wait. I wasn't even nervous about talking in front of all those people anymore. Nothing mattered but Cam and the fact that he was in the process of asking me to spend the rest of my life with him.

"Yes, yes, yes, yes, yes," I said, slowly, but while smiling and looking straight at him.

He laughed as he stood up to let me walk into his arms.

Everyone cheered like we were the prince and princess of the land, and they all approved wholeheartedly of us getting married and living happily ever after (at least that's how I'll choose to remember it). They did cheer, though. People took pictures, and we kissed, and everything was right with the world.

We had talked about getting married sooner than later, but I had not been expecting this at all. Cam had some of my coworkers collaborate on the idea, and they had come up with a drawing that was spot-on with my style. I went on and on about what a trip it was to see one of my own drawings, only to have it register that it was one that I hadn't done.

About half of the guests cleared out soon after the proposal, but others stayed, and we had a nice evening catching up with friends. All of the art sold except for a few, which Cam had already claimed.

It was after 10 when we decided to head home. Wynn and Ryan were the last ones there with us, and the four of us walked out of the gallery together.

"I love this one," Wynn said as we headed toward the door.

I looked at her to find that she was gesturing to the one I'd done of a girl walking on a path with two clay pots—one broken and one whole.

"It's gorgeous. I love all the color in those flowers," she said. I hadn't even told her the story, but she walked over to the drawing and stared at it as if it really intrigued her and she couldn't leave without seeing it one last time.

Cam, who knew the whole story about the broken pot, held me close with his arm around my shoulder as we waited for Wynn.

"I'll go ahead and take this one, too," she said, as she turned.

"Sorry," Cam said, shaking his head. "That one's mine."

The End
(till book 5)

Thanks to my team ~ Chris, Jan, and Glenda

CPSIA information can be obtained at www.ICGtesting.com
Printed in the USA
LVOW11s2305121016

508552LV00002B/129/P